Friends
More Will and Magna Stories

FRIENDS
More Will And Magna Stories

Stephen Dixon

Santa Maria

19  90

Asylum Arts

Acknowlegements

The author and the publisher wish to express their grateful acknowledgement to the following periodicals in which these stories first appeared: "Magna as a Child" and "Only the Cat Escapes" in *South Carolina Review*; "Cooked Goose" in *Florida Review* and *Grub Street*; "Friends" in *Fiction International*; "Magna as the Good Woman" in *Chouteau Review*; "pp. 201-204" in *Asylum*; "Training to Magna" in *Telescope*; "Finished" in *Poet & Critic*; "Magna Out of Earshot" in *Corona*; "Will the Writer" in *Other Voices*.

Library of Congress Catalog Number 90-080160
ISBN No. 1-878580-19-1

Cover woodcut by Francisco Franco, 1921, Paris.

Asylum Arts Publishing
P. O. Box 6203
Santa Maria, CA 93456

Contents

To Patricia L. Dixon

FRIENDS

MORE WILL AND MAGNA STORIES

To Jonathan
Very best to you always
Stephen Dixon
3 15 90

Magna As A Child

She gets on a train. A man makes a pass at her. "Hiya doing, darling?" She gets off the train. She waits on the platform. Another man comes over and says "Pardon me, young lady, but which way is up-town?"

"*This* the downtown side, that what you mean?"

"This is the downtown? That's the one I want. This the local side of the platform?"

"That's the local side there. This is the express."

"That's the one I want. The express. I have to get downtown in a hurry. Terrific business deal—you can't be-lieve it. You're too young to understand that though."

"I suppose so."

She looks away from him, stands there, holds a book bag. She knows the man's a character. It happens so often. Men want to touch her on the subway, talk to her. They follow her on the street sometimes, and certainly give her looks wher-ever she goes. One took her hand the other week, held it gently enough, and said "Why don't you come home with me. It's a nice home. A really big apartment—anything you want in it could be yours. Antiques: they're yours. Not all, of course, but some, and the more valuable the better, far as I'm concerned. Lamps, chairs, dishes—anything of these is yours. Which one of those would you like?" "Do you mind?" she said, taking her hand from his. "No, really, I'm telling the truth. Whatever you want you can have. Lamps and

chairs. Dishes too. All of them. Curtains. Brocaded curtains.
Lazy Susans. Silent butlers. Know what those are? I got two,
both sterling silver, engraved, but you can't tell what the
initials are they're engraved so fancily. Whatever you want.
You're that beautiful. Beautiful as a princess. You are a
princess. What country you a princess of, beautiful young
lady?" She had to walk across the street to get rid of him.

This one stands beside her. She knows he doesn't have
to go uptown or down. He just wants to be with her. If not
her, then another attractive girl. She knows he wants to be
on the same train with her. She has an idea he's going to sit
beside her on the train, talk to her and then get off with her
at her stop and follow her on the street or walk beside her.
She has this problem. Not a problem really, but because of
her looks she attracts strange men like this, old and young,
and they cause her problems. She happens to be very pretty.
That's not being egotistical to admit it. People have told her
it, and some have said, when she's said she's not that pretty,
"Come on. You're gorgeous, don't deny it." But she's so
young. Not even fourteen. Developed like a girl of eighteen
maybe, and maybe older. Anyway, developed. And tall for
her age. She might have already reached her full height.
And men like her for her build and face. Young face, with
very smooth clear skin, and her long blonde hair. They like
her hair. They often tell her about her hair, just as they
comment to one another or tell her about her breasts, behind
and legs. Here comes the train.

"Our train," the man says.

"Maybe just yours. I just realized I should take the local.
It's a local stop I'm going to." She goes to the other side of the
platform. The express comes. He doesn't get on it. All the
people who got off it go up the stairs or wait on her side of the
platform for the local. He comes over to her.

"The local, that's right," he says. "I have to take the

local—I forgot. What stop you taking it to?"

"Excuse me," and she walks to the end of the platform. If there's a policeman around she'll stand by him. If the man comes over to her then, she'll report the man. If the local comes and he doesn't get on it, she'll get on. If he gets on, she won't.

But there's no policeman. The man's coming toward her. That's it, she's had enough. Who should she report him to? Nobody really looks that safe or nice to talk to. She'll report him to that elderly man there, but when she gets closer to him she thinks he might be a derelict. That woman over there then.

"Excuse me, ma'am, but I'm having some trouble with that man there. He's been bothering me."

"What can I do for you, honey? Go upstairs. Tell the change clerk."

"If I can just stand with you I don't think he'll bother me anymore."

"Then I'm the one he might bother. Listen, honey, do what I say. Go upstairs, speak to the clerk in the booth. You want me to do it for you? I think I can in the time the next train comes."

"I don't want to be left down here with him. Can we go up together?"

"Better that you do it alone, honey. Maybe he won't follow. If he does I'll say something, but I don't want to miss my train."

She starts upstairs. The man starts up the stairs after her. She turns to him. The woman has her back to them, is looking down the tracks for the train. "Will you leave me alone, you crazy?"

He sticks his hand into his fly and pulls out his penis. He waves it at her. "Big, huh, and it's not even hard. Take a lick, kid. All you want. Free on the house and nobody here will mind. Go on, take a lick of it. It tastes real good."

She runs upstairs. He goes downstairs.

"That's awful," she hears the woman say, "just awful. What are you doing that for to that poor girl?"

Maybe he says or does something. By this time she's upstairs and she runs out of the station.

She comes home from her art lesson. Her mother says "Hello, sweetheart, have a nice day?" and kisses her cheek. She says she had a rotten day, maybe her worst except for when she was very sick. Her mother says "Here, let's sit down and talk."

"I don't have to sit down. I can't. I'm jumpy again just thinking about it. The art class wasn't bad—that's not it. Or not *that* bad. We had a live female model for once. Me, the big-shot, had been asking for one since they had the male model—"

"I didn't know you had male models. In the nude?"

"Sure, except for a strap down there, but when we finally got a female I almost died when I saw her body—a woman for the first time like that. It honestly scared me."

"Was she wearing drawers or something?"

"No—only he did, the male, though his behind cheeks showed. And when he bent over to make the towel under him right, one testicle showed too, someone said—though I wasn't looking at the time because I had a feeling it'd happen. But the women don't. And when she undressed in the booth she didn't even pull the curtain, nor when she got dressed again. I think she should have. There were lots of boys my age too."

"I think she should have also. Complain to the teacher. You don't want to, I will, but I think you're old enough to complain when you think something's wrong. You do enough home. But tell me, sweetheart, what was it that scared you about her so?"

"I didn't know women could get so big down there and different from me too."

"You know what you look like?"

"I've held a mirror to it. A teacher—in Hygiene—suggested us to."

"The model probably had babies. Don't let it scare you. You have plenty of time yet, and maybe she was also a little messy."

"And, well, I know what you're going to say, but I almost got molested on the subway going to Art. A man showed his penis."

"He exposed himself? Maybe you shouldn't take those classes anymore."

"No, I got away okay, I swear it, and since it was the first time ever, I don't think it'll happen again."

"I don't like it. Let me talk it over with Papa. But it was quite a day for genitalia for you. If you were old enough I'd advise your having a real drink. What about some cocoa or milk? I'll warm some for you."

"No, I'll be okay. You need help with dinner?"

"You're not just trying to bury it? You do feel better now that you got it out by telling me it?"

"Yes, Mom, yes. I won't let that experience with the man warp my future sexual and married life."

"That's a smart girl. Because he's destroyed, don't let you be."

Magna makes the salad, sets the table, does her homework, has supper, is told by her father to stay off the subways from now on unless she's traveling with someone, reads a novel she got out of the library last week with eleven other novels. She wants to read three novels a week for the next month. She thinks her mind needs it. She finished two this week and is almost done with this one—*Barchester Towers*, the longest and most boring of the three, or just the one whose language, style and consanguinity, as her teacher would say—she thinks that's the right word—but anyway, she got this far with it and if she doesn't finish it she'll be behind schedule. Then a friend calls.

"Magna," Sarah says, "I'm in love."

"Do tell me about it."

"Act more excited. It's big big news."

"Oh, do tell me about it."

"A boy in my school."

"Oh, a boy?"

"Don't be funny. A very tall masculine boy. He proposed to me today. Actually got on his knee. I said 'Get up, jerko, unless you want to be there for the next five years.' For in five years I should know, shouldn't I?"

"Am I believing this? Okay, I'm believing this. He just wants to get in your pants, Sarah. What's his name?"

"Not true and his name's Toby."

"Sounds like a clown. Drop him. No clowns allowed. Only serious names and serious professions. Charles, Henry, Ernest. Statesmen, physicians, writers, composers, choreographers, painters. Especially painters and all those in the plastic arts."

"Magna, you're too staid. You also should have a boyfriend."

"I almost did on the subway today. Listen to this. A man wanted to take me home. Said he'd give me anything. For starters, he showed me his penis."

"No."

"Actually, that was another one last week. Nothing exposed. This one today—and he was my second potential boyfriend in three minutes. The first on the subway went goo-goo with his eyes till I thought they'd pop out—but this one, well, he brought his thing out and said— Wait, are my folks around? No. He said 'Lick.' I could have killed him. He was insane. If I had a gun I would have shot it off—truly."

"You wouldn't."

"Maybe not, but I've been thinking, isn't there something they can do for men like that? Women too if they jump all over boys our age the same way? Oh, boys wouldn't mind. They're dumb enough to think it's great and they're so attractive if any woman suddenly pulled out her breast to them and said 'Suck, eat, crunch, squeeze.' But men. Maybe they could show them pictures of rats eating garbage same time they show them pictures of little and big girls."

"Good idea. We can show these films in movie theaters. We can charge admission and make lots of money."

"I'm speaking of photographs, not movies, and you're missing my point besides."

"I'm not. Magna, you're getting too serious for me. But what did it look like this rope he had?"

"If you mean by rope, big, or if you're just using it as another word for any sized penis—"

"Was it ugly, I mean? Sounds as if it would be. With bumps and scales on it and disease leaking out."

"All of that. What do you think, I took time to stare? I felt sorry for him at first and also that he was very depraved, but most of all I was scared."

"So you admit that?"

"Sarah, why wouldn't I?"

"I don't know. I had nothing else to say. But you want to hear about Harry? That's my new flame."

"What happened to Toby?"

"Toby is what I wish his name was. I know you don't like it, but I do."

"Okay, okay, so long as your story doesn't have genitals

in it. I'm tired of that today."

"Harry wouldn't do that. He might want to one day—
with me, in a nice way, no creep flashing his raincoat on the
street, I mean—but that's some day, not today. I met him in
the lunchroom. In a half-hour I knew he was it. He waited
for me after school. Already sound too good to be true? He
escorted me—that's the word he used—if he could; you
know—to my ballet class."

"I like the word escort. He's sounding good. He have a
friend?"

"He says he has a few and they're all almost as nice as he
is. Harry's not modest. He also plays the cello."

"My favorite instrument."

"If that's so I won't let you near him. I told him the cello
was the most beautiful instrument in the world, but I don't
like any string sound but the guitar. And the mandolinski."

"Why the ski?"

"To give it a, well, a little Russian flavor. Because I love
Russian everything—Russian dancing and Russian dan-
cers especially. I've changed my name to ski, you know.
Sarah Nortonski."

"Okayski, Miss Nortonski, any other newski?"

"Yes. You can sleep over this Friday. Mom says it's all
right. And you know my dad didn't mind, since he has a
crush on you."

"Sure he does."

"He does. He says 'How's your friend Magna? How come
we see so little of her these days? Let me tell you,' he tells me,
'if I was a young woman of fourteen and wanted a good friend
for life, Magna's the one I'd choose.' Other times he's called
you beautiful, witty, charming, precocious—I love that. And
brilliant, he once said—talented and brilliant and, my dear,
what extraordinary poise. That's how he put it. He's in love
with you, you cookie."

"Then think I want to sleep over your house?"

"Oh, he's in love with my mother also, but he's got a Russian crusher on you. You deserve it too. You're really everything he says."

"Why thank you, Ski. Sure I can come Friday. But I have to clear it with my folks. Hold on."

Magna goes into the livingroom. Her father says "I don't see why not," and her mother says "Let me speak to Mrs. Norton." The two women talk. The girls are both dears and a pleasure to have over, the mothers agree, and Friday will be fine.

"Great," Sarah says to Magna. "I can't wait. I'm going with Harry to a movie on Saturday or I would've asked you for that night too."

"Is he staying over Saturday?"

"Magna, how could you? This is an extension. And of course he's not. You know that."

"I'm sorry, that was dumb of me. Okay, got to run, unless you have other important news."

"How about you? I always talk, you never do."

"What I told you about Mr. Subway wasn't talking? And I saw a woman completely nude for the first time in my life today in art class. I suffered and I know why too. I'm going to end up looking like her, with my breasts and hips already large as they are. I don't think I'll have as much hair down there as she had, or I hope not, and never mounds of it under my arms and so dark, nor will I look so down and out, and so sad. But the body has to end up sagging like that, doesn't it?"

"Not with us dancers, my dear. Keeps the breasts and tushies tight—not just the legs. Ever see some of the old ones? Sixty, seventy years old. I've seen them in the showers and dressing rooms at ballet school and their bodies still look half great."

"Maybe I should give up painting for dancing then, but aren't we talking silly? Always the body, never the mind."

"Not you, just me. I can't stand to think deep or read. All I ever want to do with my life is eat like an amazon and exercise and dance. Oh: see ballets and good ballet rehearsals too. But you're getting much too serious for me, and I got to scoot too. See you Friday, Brainstein, and come straight from school."

In bed that night she thinks about the model. The teacher told the class to go up and take a good look at her. "It's allowed. I checked beforehand with Astor and she said for the sake of art and higher learning, look anywhere you like and close as you want too, though keep a five feet distance from her if you have a bad cold."

Magna stayed on her stool, drawing the model and the few students who went up to look at her. The teacher came up behind her and said "What're you concocting there, a basket of fruit? Take advantage—go up and give her a real inspection, unless it's against your principles or whatever, of course."

"It's not. It's just that, you know, I'm a little concerned she might think I'm just staring, no matter what you said she said. And I thought I had a pretty good drawing going till you came by, but if you still—" He was nodding his head, so she put the drawing down and went up to the model.

The model was on the floor on her back, legs spread apart, looking up at the wall clock. Magna stared at several parts of her body—hand, feet, shoulders—before she looked between her legs. It's so shiny and big. They're really not the prettiest things in the world, that's for sure, though penises, from what she's seen of them on statues and in photographs, aren't the nicest looking things either and look stupid besides. But go back and draw it. Let Mr. Finkel think "Oh boy, this kid really got something from my lesson—maybe more, if she shows it to her folks, than I bargained for."

She made a large drawing of just the model's legs spread apart and her vagina and pubic area. Mr. Finkel came over, made believe he was handing her something and said "Here, kid, you get today's cigar. It's your best effort yet, not just for what you put in but what you left out also." She said "I think I know what you mean, but can you explain it further?" He said "Just think about it—you'll get it," and walked away. She still didn't know what he meant and doubted he did either. Just pretending to be profound, like most of her teachers, but anyway...

She's been rubbing herself down there for the last few minutes. Door's closed and lights out and she's under the covers. She's tried to masturbate a few times but has either fallen asleep doing it or stopped because she thought one of her parents might walk in and turn the light on at the same time and catch her at it, and once when the light was on she thought there might be a tiny hole in the ceiling or walls someplace and one of her parents or the building's tenants might be looking through it. She knows where and how to rub and what she's supposed to do to complete it. She's read a couple of library books about it and what the end's supposed to be like, but she's never come near to feeling anything but a little titillation down there while she was doing it. She also read in one of those books that every woman, including married ones, should practice masturbation for all sorts of reasons—spiritual, political, like that— and sooner a younger woman learns how, better it'll be for her and all freedom-loving women in general, so she's never really felt much guilt over it but hasn't yet talked about it with anyone. She doesn't like the idea she's doing it so soon after she saw that man on the subway, but is sure that incident had nothing to do with it. In fact, more she thinks of him, less interested she is in continuing to rub herself, so she closes and opens her eyes a few times to get him out of her head, and also changes hands because the right one's become tired. The model today probably had more to do with it than anything else. Thinking of that woman's vagina probably made her think of her own, though without really knowing it, since right after she thought of her she found her hand rubbing down there. Sarah and her new boyfriend and the heavy petting she bets they'll start doing in a month if they stay together? No, she never thought of that till now, though again that's not to say somewhere deep inside she hadn't been thinking of it. But she still doesn't think so, nor anything related to Sarah's father being infatuated with her, something she already knew by his actions and looks and wishes he'd stop, more for her friendship with Sarah and Sarah's mother's sake than her own. Anyway, whatever it was that started her doing it, it's not working. She's been rubbing for around fifteen minutes, both hands are tired, she's beginning to ache down there from it, and she's no further along in getting excited as those books said she'd get than she was a few seconds after she started. Maybe she's doing it wrong or is just too young yet or the books left out something or some other reason. No big deal. It was more out of curiosity that she wanted to complete it than any other thing. She turns on the light, listens from her bed if anyone's behind the door, reads a little and falls asleep.

In one of her dreams there was a big bull with a long unicorn's horn on its head. She knows what those mean and knew in the dream. In the dream she said to the bull, when he stepped out from behind a bush and got into a charging position, "Come on, I know what you and that horn mean. You want to try and fool me with symbols and stuff, get more complicated, but don't come around like some old-time figure in art." She's become something of an expert on her dreams. Her youngest aunt's a psychotherapist and they've talked about their dreams a lot. The bull chased her after she lectured him on dreams and art. That was when she stopped interpreting within the dream, or even thought of it as one, and it became more like a normal dream. She was dressed only in white, even her socks and shoes. White's such an obvious symbol for her, though she didn't think of it then, but it can also stand for death, can't it?—in the Orient her aunt's said and she's read. Anyway, she was chased, fell back against a wall that had a few pillows on it, that suddenly became one huge pillow. A bed, what else? or something close to it. No? Yes. The bull charged from about ten feet away, head down, horn out, straight at her. She thought she'd be pierced by the horn and she screamed, so loud that she thinks she must have screamed outside of the dream too. The horn was a few inches from her stomach when she woke.

She's thirsty. She gets up and goes to the kitchen for some ice water or seltzer. Her mother's reading in the livingroom. "Everything all right, sweetheart? It's past two."

"I had a bad dream. Did you hear me scream?"

"No. It was that bad? Anything you want to talk about?"

"I don't know if it was that bad, just very revealing, I think."

"Tell me."

"I dreamt about a man about to penetrate me with an erection. In the stomach. But it's the same thing, isn't it—myself down there and my stomach? Only the man was a bull with a unicorn's horn, and the horn, well it has to be what I think it is to think it was an erection, right?"

"Sounds right. You haven't had any of those experiences—even close to it—have you?"

"Me? Not a chance. How would I? Where?"

"I'm not accusing you, I'm just naturally worried. So it

was your whole day of bad experiences today. But anything else bothering you related to sex?"

"I don't know about bothering me, but another man got suggestive with me on the subway, right before the one who exposed himself. I just walked away."

"Maybe from now on let's take the bus."

"And Sarah's father. I didn't want to say anything for I don't want to hurt my friendship with her, but if she's telling the truth, he has a crush on me. Actually I know he has. I've seen the way he looks."

"You think you're old enough to tell?"

"I am. And not that he's evil or would do anything or anything, but he doesn't do a good job of hiding it."

"Then maybe you shouldn't sleep over there this Friday after all."

"Maybe for a while it's not a good idea. I can go over for afternoons and she can sleep here."

"Don't tell her the reasons though. It'd only hurt her. So, sweetheart, back to sleep?"

"I also tried to masturbate tonight and not for the first time too. That's all right also, considering everything, isn't it? I didn't want to tell you, but we were talking and I guess I really wanted to get it out, and now it is."

"What can I say? That I like hearing it? Not so much. The act itself is normal for young women as well as some older ones, I suppose—I'm not going to say at what specific age you do and you don't—but let's not talk about it anymore. It's not that nonsense that I don't like learning you're growing up but maybe something you can try to save for your friends. But if anything is troubling you and you want to talk about it, no matter what it is, come to your father or me or both. Now off to bed."

"I want to get something cold to drink first."

"Not too cold or you'll have trouble sleeping."

Magna pours herself a glass of seltzer. Her mother goes back to her reading. Later her mother comes into Magna's room, thinks she's sleeping, pulls the covers up an inch or two to Magna's neck.

Cooked Goose

They said no more stories, no more novels, we don't want anything of yours anymore, your novels don't sell, your collections do even worse, each of your books gets panned more than the last one, find another publisher if you can but you'll be wasting your time and ours if you send another work in.

I phone several editors at different publishing houses and they all say the same thing. They've read my reviews and sometimes my stories and books and I should feel lucky I even got my work published and reviewed. Try another profession—that's our advice. If you feel you must be in the arts, try music or mixed media or something like that—acting, because occasionally your dialogue hits the mark, for about three sentences in a row, but please don't bother sending us any of your manuscripts.

I write a short story and think this is one of my best and send it to a magazine and finish the novel I've been writing for a year and make a few copies of it and send these to publishers and begin another novel and write more stories and send these to magazines and I get back rejection slips and letters from magazine and book editors all saying please don't try us again, be so kind as to solicit beforehand whether we want to read your work, your fiction is not only unsalable but just plain unworthy—the syntax and bad taste, the characters, the grammar, style, form, content, language, writing, wording, everything, you're deceiving yourself, you're taking up our valuable time which we could much better be using to read novels and collections by other writers—our own and newer writers we've asked to send their work in.

I finish the novel and send the two new novels out and write more stories and another novel, which is the third part of the trilogy to the last two novels, and send this work out separately to some publishers and all three together to other publishers and the few literary agents I haven't tried yet and my stories to magazines and anthologies and a collection of my last twenty stories to other publishers and they all return my work saying just about the same thing. This isn't for us and we don't see any other house publishing it either. You're fooling yourself and should get out of writing fiction or at least take a couple years break from it. You had a professional writing career going once but something happened along the way to stop it that is probably as unexplainable to you as it is to us, even if it isn't that rare. Maybe you should try finding a job in journalism or advertising, publishing, publicity or technical or medical writing. If you feel you have to make a living doing fiction, try writing a popular novel. Something about outer space or a detective or erotic novel or a book for kids—anything but what you're writing now which we know was intended to be serious fiction but just doesn't come across at all that way.

Manuscripts come back and I continue to write. I finish another story collection in a year and my fourth novel in two years. The fourth novel continues where the trilogy left off, so I now not only have another novel to send around but also a tetralogy. Comments come back with my manuscripts. I start a new novel. Royalty checks from the early promising works of mine have stopped coming in. Anthologies that carried my early stories are now out of print. I am out of money. Utility companies are threatening to shut off my gas, lights and phone. My landlord says tough as he knows life has been for me over the past ten years, he'll have to have my six months back rent or throw me out. I'm evicted. A city marshall breaks down my door and takes all my furniture and clothes away to sell for whatever he can get from them to pay back part of my rent. I try to keep my typewriter but two of the marshall's assistants pull it out of my hands. A locksmith puts new locks on my door and laughs when I ask for a set of the new keys. I'm left with several shopping bags of my manuscripts and what's in my pockets.

I sit on the front stoop of the building I lived in. The mailman comes, doesn't see my name on the letterbox anymore and drops a few envelopes of returned manuscripts on my lap and says goodluck. A woman brings me a sandwich and glass of water and says "I've heard you typing for years across the air shaft and wondered what you were writing— term papers for university students, hate letters to the mayor—but never figured it for fiction till the mailman just told me it was. I've always admired creative people in all fields and they have to eat no matter how much they're nourished by their pursuits, isn't that so?"

"They also need a place to live and work in, so would you please by any chance have a spare room for free for a couple months till I really get back on my feet?"

"That I think would be carrying my support for the arts a little too far," and when I tell her I'm not hungry for her food now though do thank her for it, she takes the plate and glass home with her, leaving the sandwich in one of my shopping bags.

Night comes. I suddenly get a good idea for a short story. I take a pen and pad out of my pocket and begin writing it. A policeman pulls up in a car when I'm halfway through the story and says the landlord and a few tenants and neighbors complained about my sitting on the stoop for so long and looking a bit seedy with all those bags and my worn work clothes, so I'll have to move.

I cross the street and sit on the sidewalk curb and finish the story. It's the first story I've written entirely by hand in twenty years. I tried to keep the writing neat and pages clean but it still doesn't look too good. The pen ran out of ink and when I continued to write the story by pencil, lead smudges along with my fingerprints soiled several pages.

I take one of the envelopes from my returned manuscripts, cross off my name on the front and write the name and address of a popular magazine and put the story in it and drop it in a mailbox. It probably won't get there without stamps and if it does and the magazine pays the postage due on the envelope rather than handing it back to the mailman, it probably won't get accepted, but you never know. The magazine might think it the best story I've sent them and give me a good deal of money for it and a contract to get first look at every story I write for the next few years. It's happened to other writers who have placed stories in that magazine and I never thought their work was any better than mine.

Suddenly an idea comes to me. The streetlight's bad where I sit and the weather's gotten windy and cold, so I find a quiet-enough bench at the bus terminal and begin a new novel that has no relationship to the last four. I write all night and the following day, nibbling on my sandwich sparingly to keep away debilitating hunger for as long as I can, and think this novel might end up being the best one I've written so far.

Friends

They're sitting at a bar. Floyd says "I have to tell you something, now that you brought up Gabe—something you might not want to hear."

"What, that he doesn't like it that I didn't like his novel?"

"He told me about it. It hurts him very much. Not that you didn't like it but that you dropped him cold right after it was published, without even writing him about the book when he sent you a copy."

"He stole parts of it from one of my novels. I once—do you know the story?"

"He never mentioned anything about it. He just feels you couldn't face it or something that he got a book out before you, and because you still haven't published one, it's still bothering you."

"Listen. He was once over my place for dinner with his girlfriend Pearl."

"Pearl. Boy, that name brings back memories. Floods. But what happened?"

"He lived downtown then—well, still does, but at that time a block away from White Nights Press. So I asked if he'd drop my manuscript off—my novel *Flowers*, which was new then but I've since trunked."

"That's right. She got married, to a doctor, has a kid, Gabe said."

"Did she? Pearl? Anyway, I didn't want to send the novel

fourth class—it could take two weeks in this city—and first class would cost a few bucks."

"So he took it to them for you."

"Eventually. But that night, around two a.m., I couldn't believe it, phone rings—"

"Gabe calling saying how much he likes your novel."

"He told you?"

"No, that's just the way he is and always has been. Gets a manuscript, starts reading—can't keep his hands off it, really—and if it's good, and I'm assuming yours was, and he's too tired to finish it but wants more time to—a few hours after he wakes up the next day when he's supposed to be bringing it to the publisher, let's say. That what happened?"

"Truth is, he didn't even have to call me about it. He could've brought it to them the day after the next—what would be the difference? It'd still be getting to White Nights earlier than it would if I sent it by mail."

"But he was trying to give you confidence. Trying to say—saying it for all I know—and you must have been flattered and felt good and so on he called, even if he woke you up—that he likes it, he, another writer, and so much so that he's asking for more time so he can finish it—time when he would normally be writing himself."

"Sure he liked it and needed more time. Liked it enough to steal from it and needed more time to photocopy or type parts of it. Not whole paragraphs and sentences. But two or three characters and several ideas and scenes, all changed a little, and a lot of dialogue changed even less—but distinctive dialogue, not hello and goodbye dialogue; but idiosyncratic dialogue."

"That he never said. None of it."

"Of course not. Why would he?"

"Still, why didn't you at least say thanks for the complimentary copy of his book? 'Congratulations'—after all, it was his first published book—and that you were reading it. Then, maybe some day later after you had really done some comparison research on the two novels, taken him up on the parts you thought he swiped."

"You still don't see why I dropped him cold?"

"I see, I see, from your perspective, but you don't know what you did to him. And the guy's in such awful physical state that I also don't want to see him emotionally hurt. I in fact want to see him emotionally built up. But maybe, to be fair to both of you, the important thing to ask you now is how much time elapsed between his taking your manuscript to White Nights—I assume they weren't that interested in it if it was never published."

"I said so, they rejected it, not even a peep. Just 'Thanks very much'—not even saying they'll be glad to look at my next novel if there's one, which editors usually say. Now I don't care—then I did. I don't even know if I like it anymore, and I've stolen parts of it, consciously or unconsciously, out of it myself."

"Any of the parts that you say ended up in Gabe's book?"

"Some, and also the idea that he took from my novel. Put it into another novel. But there I said sentence for sentence what Abe, a character who's very much like Gabe, took from the narrator's manuscript, which the narrator then had to trunk. That novel was sent all around too."

"White Nights see it?"

"Sure. Also the same editor Gabe had at his publisher, but if he recognized anything, he never said it. But what do you think I should do with Gabe now? After four years of not talking to him since he sent me his book, I should write him about it, give him a call, apologize?"

"It'd be nice. And without saying you thought he stole from your novel. Anyway, by this time you should just forget that."

"No, I couldn't write or call him about that book. It still sticks in my throat."

"Want another drink?"

"I think I've had it."

"Dave," Floyd says to the bartender, "another for me, a fresh soda in back; I think he's finished. —So, do me a favor and yourself one too. He's more than just sick. He's deteriorated pitifully in the last two years. By the way he looks and what someone said the doctors say about him, he isn't going to last another year. He's too weak most days to leave his apartment and some days to leave his bed. He's living off Welfare and Medicare and what money the writing organizations give him from their emergency funds. But still trickling out his fiction—not getting any of it published—and some articles for the *Voice*."

"I've seen them. Throwbacks to the Fifties and Sixties."

"He's only writing them for money and to keep his name in print, so he'd mostly agree with you. But call him, don't write. Say you just read his book a second time and realize what a shit you've been about it all these years. You don't have to explain. Just talk about how good's his book. He's been carrying this sore for a long time and it'll make him happy. And you know, outside of what you say he did to you, I've never heard anything but the best things about what he's done for others."

"I don't have a copy. I gave mine away after I read it."

"So what? All I want you to do is praise. Call him now, in fact. From the phone over there. While I drink, you call. He loves your work, you know."

"Does he? What's he looking for, another of my unpublished manuscripts?"

"Don't be mean. He likes your work a lot and feels lousy you still haven't a book out. And he's done what he could for you—without telling you and despite your silence; even wrote several book editors in your behalf, he said. That was nice of him. Most writers don't go out of their way for other writers like that—you've said so yourself."

"He sort of owes it to me, no? Because I'd say fifty pages of that six-hundred-page book of his had some of my stuff in it—that's why I stopped sending my novel around. I thought anyone who had read his book—"

"Not many did, so little chance of that."

"But if someone had, he'd have said he'd read something like this before—parts of it—and word might have got around that I plagiarized Gabe's book and then no publisher would have looked at my work again."

"You got them down as too scrupulous. Anyway, it's over, past—illness makes it over if anything—so call him now, because if you don't, you never will. What do you say?"

"I hate that he's so sick, but calling him still isn't easy."

"Come on."

"Okay."

He goes to the back and dials Gabe's number. Gabe answers weakly. "It's Will, Gabe—long time no talk and all that—but how's it going?"

"How's it going? Will who? Not Taub."

"The same. Haven't changed my name."

"Well I'll be. I thought you were dead."

"You mean you wished I was dead."

"Actually, I knew you weren't and of course I'd never wish it. Floyd says he keeps running into you—I bet it was he who told you to call."

"Truth is, that's true. You know me—could never tell a lie. He said you weren't feeling too good, which I'm very sorry about—I hate to see anybody I know sick—so I'm calling. Look, he also said something I'm not supposed to say to you—"

"That I was angry you never wrote me about my first

book. That it hurt me."

"Right. Listen, I'm sorry. If you can keep this a secret between us two—meaning, not tell Floyd I said this, because he'll only think I was trying to hurt you again, which I'm not, believe me, I'm not—I didn't write you then because I was mad as hell at you for lifting certain scenes and dialogue and even two characters from my own novel *Flowers*."

"*Flowers?*"

"Come on, you know the one. The novel I asked you to bring to White Nights because you lived around the corner from them then. And you called up that night—early in the morning, really—"

"Oh yeah. But you thought I stole from that piece of crap? You've got to be mistaken. If I'm going to steal from something—"

"'Crap'? You called me at two or three in the morning—it's what I'm talking about—and said you loved it—loved the first hundred pages of it, at least—as much as anything you've read of anyone's in the last ten years—and could I give you another half day to finish it."

"I said that? Bull. It's true I started to read it—on the subway home that night. I was with Pearl—remember Pearl?"

"Floyd said she got married and had a kid."

"Sure she got married. To a rich man—the kind she always wanted, the whore. I hope she's unhappy. Not the baby, but just she. She's a bitch—was, is, always will be."

"I thought she was kind of nice. Almost too good for you, if you want to know what I felt then. Too good for me too, if I can be—"

"Too good for anyone. A goddamn snob. Good riddance to her forever. I've known ten better women since. Prettier, better, smarter—everything. But about your piece of trash *Flowers*, if that was its title. So that's what you must tell people why you cut me off flat. Well let me tell you, baby, I read twenty pages of that manuscript on the subway home—if you ever see that bitch Pearl again, ask her. She'll corroborate, if she hasn't also become a liar, that I thought it trash then and wanted to toss it out the train window— even made believe I was going to and she had to grab my arm to stop me—not that I'd go that far. You would have killed me. But I read about twenty pages and told her that anyone who could write this badly will never be able to write well in his entire life. And I still think it. Your work since—what I've seen of it in small magazines—stinks. God only knows why they print it. Just tells me what I've thought all along about them—the little magazines have no taste, it's all in and who you know and the rest of that crap."

"You're just saying this because you're too damn ashamed—did I say ashamed? I mean you're too damn gutless to admit that you lifted from my manuscript. You read the whole thing all right. You had to to steal one of the characters who doesn't appear till my novel's last scene. You even stole that idea."

"What idea?"

"That a character—an important one to the denouement of the novel—"

"Oh, 'denouement' now. Big words from a small mind."

"—doesn't appear till the very last scene in your novel. But whole sections lifted. Dialogue—almost word for word sometimes. The way your main character made love to his wife—every Saturday, exactly at midnight, while my main character did it every day but Sunday and exactly at eleven. And that both our couples always used the same position when they made love—yours not much different from mine—and that the girlfriend in my novel would never take off her earrings in bed while the wife in your novel wouldn't take off her stockings or socks."

"What, you invented all the sex in the world—you invented the clock? The clock's been invented and so have all the positions and sexual peculiarities and hang-ups."

"Listen, this phone conversation is a bust. You know what I'm saying but you're intentionally distorting it to protect yourself. I'm sorry you're ill and I hope—and this is the truth—you get well again and sooner the better, but somehow your lousy situation right now isn't enough to make me forgive you for what you did."

"Bull and more bull. You're just angry, and are also trying to do some double number on me when you couldn't get me to admit to the first, because your own novel wasn't good enough to get published, just as none of your longer works have been. While at least one of my fat novels, which was equal in size to about three of your midgets, not only got published but by a major house. For you know damn well I never lifted anything from you. If I did take a line or word or two from the first twenty pages, then it was subconscious. But I doubt even that happened because I think everything in those first twenty pages wasn't good enough to take."

"Again, I hope you get better, Gabe, and I'm sorry for the tough time you've had recently, but I also think you're a liar and a thief. Goodbye," and he hangs up.

"So, how'd it go?" Floyd says, handing Will a drink. "I knew you'd need one after your call, so I ordered a brandy for you—French and straight up."

"Thanks. I do need it. How'd it go? Okay. He sounded weak in the very beginning but then his voice got really robust. I told him I reread his book and liked it and he said thanks. But everything overall, he doesn't seem well."

"Did he give you the business about his living another ten years but not later than that?"

"Something like it, I think."

"He's imagining it. I've had a couple of discussions about

him with his last live-in, Cecily."

"I don't think I knew that one."

"You wouldn't have. She dropped him about half a year
ago—moved out, they were battling all the time—but still
comes over with food and things and clean laundry sometimes. She said the doctors definitely think—but I mentioned this before, didn't I?—oh damn," and he starts crying.
He wipes his eyes with his bar napkin, then his face with his
handkerchief.

"Yeah, you told me. I'm sorry. I can't say the world of
letters is losing a great writer—I shouldn't even talk about
it that way. He's a good writer and once was very good, but
the world in general is just, well, losing a very nice guy,
mostly. Whatever, it's just awful when someone so young–"

"It's disgraceful. A cure will be found for his
disease–you'll see–two to three years after he goes. It
happened with my sister and it'll happen to him. To Gabe,
right?" holding up his glass. "To Gabe Peabody, a hell of a
good writer—*still*, I think; even with the crap he has to
produce, it's still better written than most anybody's—and
let's face it, one of the most decent courageous guys around."

"I can drink to that." They drink.

"Then it's all straightened out with him?"

"Straightened out? Sure. Well. Listen, Floyd, why am I
lying to you? Lie to you, lie to everybody—I just ought to
stop. I called Gabe with good intentions, but once I heard his
voice and we started talking, I got upset about what he did
with my manuscript then. So I—"

"You didn't. Brought it up? You told him off?"

"That's what I did. I called him a thief and worse. But do
you know what he had the balls to tell me?"

"You're a bastard, do you know that? For do you realize
how sick he is? Kicking the goddamn guy like that when he's
so far down?"

"Listen, I know Gabe too and I thought he'd appreciate the truth more—or just what I was thinking more—the grudge I've held—than some b.s. about how much I liked his book. But you know what he said about my manuscript? That he never—"

"I don't want to hear. Dave," he yells to the bartender. "Please, I have to go. Will a twenty take care of it?"

Dave nods. Floyd puts two tens on the bar, gets his coat off the hook behind them and heads for the door.

"Well, I just don't think an illness, no matter how severe—" Will's saying to Floyd's back. "Oh, maybe if he was on his deathbed," but Floyd's out the door.

Will grabs his coat and runs after him. He catches up with him a half-block away. "Listen to me, Floyd—I told Gabe the truth, the truth, because the issue has been with me a long time. Because my gripe I thought was as big as his—that he stole and didn't apologize. Even bigger. That I didn't write him was the least of what I wanted to do then. I wanted to sue him. Did for a couple of years. I wanted to turn him in to every writing organization there was. You don't know—you're not a writer—what it's like to write something for two-plus years and then have some guy—a friend—copy from it left and right and make your manuscript useless."

"You could have rewritten and changed the parts you say he took from. So it would have taken awhile. But it would have saved the manuscript and for all you know, made it better. Anything can stand more work."

"He took the best parts. I would have had to change the whole tone or something. He took the spirit out of that novel or just out of me. Whatever he did, I just couldn't go back to it."

"Maybe then, but now?"

"Now it's old stuff to me. I'm doing other things in other

ways—I couldn't imitate that style anymore. That's what happens."

"You say. Maybe you should get over the idea that you can't. Anyway, you know your business, but what I want from you right now is to call him. That's right—don't look at me as if I'm nuts. There's a booth there. If the phone's working, call him and apologize. Even if you don't mean it— though you should—say you're sorry. You lost your head, you didn't mean what you said, you realize he didn't steal from your book. Maybe a line here, a word there, but so what?—and you were just drunk or something before. Not 'something'; you drank too much tonight and said those things out of some drunkenness or some blind rage against something else that's been bothering you, but it wasn't what you know is true."

"He'll know you put me up to it. I already told him you told me to call him to say what a great book he wrote—"

Floyd swings at him, grazes his forehead, lunges at him again with his arm cocked but Will steps back and walks the other way, saying with his back to Floyd "It's just what I always thought about life. Not always but for a long time. People don't want to—oh the hell with it."

"Of course they don't in certain situations, you idiot," Floyd shouts. "You bastard. You goddamn pitiless sonofabitch and your goddamn pitiless truth. Sure, keep walking, but no wonder your writing smells."

Will goes into the bar, says to Dave "If you think you don't want me in here because of the commotion I made before, tell me and I'll go."

"No, it's okay. Only don't get so loud again if you don't mind. Brandy?"

"Right. A double. Not the expensive kind Floyd ordered; just the house stuff." He drinks two doubles, turns it all over in his mind several times. Maybe I was wrong. No, I was right. Stealing from an unpublished manuscript is bad news—unforgivable if the person who stole it doesn't acknowledge it. I should call him. He should have called me. Ages ago. But I gave away Floyd's secret. So what's he complaining about? I made him look like an even nicer guy to Gabe. But Gabe's dying, Floyd says. Maybe he is. Let's say he is. No, he is—everyone says he is. They say I wouldn't recognize him even if I made an appointment to meet him someplace and he showed up at the exact spot at the right time. That he's lost maybe thirty pounds and he was always thin. All right. I did the wrong thing. I couldn't control myself. That's how I am. No, that's not good enough. Floyd was right about everything. I have to apologize to him when he gets home. Call him in five minutes. And Gabe. Call him and apologize for everything—say you were drunk—and then call Floyd and say you called Gabe and apologized just the way he asked you to.

He goes to the phone, calls Gabe. Gabe says "Yes?"

"Listen, Gabe, it's Will."

Hangs up. Calls back. "Gabe, don't hang up. I apologize. I was drunk. I'm a schmuck. I didn't mean what I said at all. I was mad about some other things and took it out on you. This woman I was seeing—she dumped me. I've been bitter and depressed about it for weeks and have been dumping on everyone since because of it."

"Whew. Nice excuse. You're a writer. Writers usually have good excuses. I should know. I've got good excuses too when I need them—to me, to the people I'm excusing myself to. Fine. I accept your apology. I accept it because I'm not a big grudgeholder and because it took a lot to call back. Floyd obviously pressured you into it, but it still took a lot."

"Floyd won't even speak to me now. He tried to slug me after I told him what I told you. But literally—threw a punch."

"Really? That's very flattering. Floyd's a good guy; you and I, we're not such good guys. Hey, I think we should talk more, Will, but now's not the time. You want to have lunch soon?"

"Sure, when? Why don't you come to my place? I'll make us something."

"I can't get around much."

"I'll send a cab and pay for it too. Call it part of my apology."

"You'd do that? My old pals are really coming through for me tonight. But you're so apologetic, so guilty. Never saw you like that."

"That's right, I am. But I'll do it. I want to forget what happened. Let's say we worked it out. Have we?"

"I think this phone conversation has done something to that effect."

"Then, and I'm saying this in all sincerity and without any animosity, admit to me something too. You stole, didn't you?"

"If I said yes, just to see what you'd say, I know you'd call me the worst names going. You're wily and changeable like that. But I'll say yes, I did steal, just to see what you'll say."

"No, the truth. Say it without those added things. Did you or did you not steal from *Flowers*? And not just a few words or sentences from it. I'm talking about whole characters and parts. You read the whole thing. You had to have."

"I read twenty, at the most thirty to thirty-five pages on the subway as I said. And skip-reading. You're asking too much to think anyone could read it any other way or read more."

"Look, I'm not going to prosecute or hold you to it after this call. It's all over. My novel's junked. I just want to know for my own satisfaction."

"And I've told you. If it doesn't satisfy you, what can I say?"

"Forget the lunch invitation."

"Think I would have come even in a chauffeured-driven car? You'd put poison in the food. For both of us. You're suicidal. You hate life because you can't write and you've never really been published and so you want to take everyone with you."

"You didn't call that night, right, to say how much you loved the first half of my novel? What did you call for—to put me off-guard?"

"What are you talking about again that I called? You're crazy, baby. See a doctor," and he hangs up.

Will calls Floyd and says "Floyd, it's me, give me a few seconds, but you know Gabe's out of his head, don't you?"

"No I don't," and he hangs up.

Will calls back and says "It's me again, I shouldn't have said what I did, but do you have Pearl's number?"

"Haven't I made it clear? I don't want to talk to you."

"All right, you don't, and no doubt for good reason, but do you have her number or the name of her husband and city they live in if she isn't in the Manhattan directory and neither of them live here?"

"They live here, I don't know if she still has her old name or is in the book. But his is Charnoff, spelled the way it sounds I'd guess, a Mt. Sinai doctor, Gabe said, and since he also teaches there and has an office on upper Fifth, I'd say he lives around there too. You going to call her and make her feel like hell too?"

"You might disagree with me, but I want to know what happened with my manuscript back then, but once and for all. I just want to know how much he read and could possibly have stolen from it. If I find out in his favor, I'll apologize up and down the line to him. To him and you—a public apology if I have to—in the sky, any place, that he wasn't out of his head but it was me."

"No you won't. Your problem is even if you find out the truth—"

"I swear it's not. Listen, I'm sorry and I know we'll be good friends again after this but probably not that soon. Goodnight." He hangs up before Floyd can say anything else, dials Information, gets Charnoff's home number and calls. Pearl answers.

"Pearl, this is Will Taub, Gabe's old friend—it's not too late to call, is it?"

"What happened? Don't tell me he died?"

"No, though he's pretty sick though, but that isn't why I called."

"How sick is he? In the hospital?"

"He's at home. You want his number? He doesn't live where he used to when you knew him, but I have it right on me."

"Why would I want his number? Last time we spoke he insulted me something awful. But I was concerned how his health was. He was killing himself the way he drank and didn't eat, not that I'd ever want to speak to him about it or anything else again. What I'm saying is, no matter what went wrong between Gabe and me, I can still have sympathy for him."

"Of course. I didn't mean anything by it. How are you, by the way?"

"I'm fine, and you?"

"Fine too. But let me tell you why I called. Did you read his novel—the only one of his published?"

"Sure. *Clash!* Why?"

"Well, it was my feeling after reading it that Gabe took a lot of material from my unpublished novel *Flowers*, which I gave him one night to bring to a publisher downtown after you two had had dinner at my place. Do you remember?"

"I think so. We went by subway. That was before I bought

my car for school."

"That's right—the subway. Well, Gabe claims he only read twenty pages of my novel and then wanted to throw it out the subway car window he thought it was so bad. Do you remember that? He said you would. Because what I remember is that later that same evening he called me up—at two or three in the morning—and told me he read half my novel so far and loved it and needed more time to finish it before he took it to the publisher, which was White Nights, though that I wouldn't expect you to remember."

"I don't remember him wanting to throw anything out the window but himself a few times."

"I'm talking about your subway ride home."

"I know, but how do you expect me to remember that? It was six years ago."

"Four years ago—five at the most."

"It's too small an incident to remember."

"Then what about Gabe calling me later in the morning—that two to three a.m. call—and telling me on the phone how much he loved my novel? Do you remember that?"

"Of course not. I was probably asleep when he called."

"Do you remember, then, before you went to bed, Gabe staying up late to read my novel, and maybe in the morning—"

"I don't remember any of that. I do remember having dinner with you and I think her name was Lucille—"

"Louise."

"Louise, Lucille—I was close. And that we took the subway home. I don't know why I remember the subway. Maybe because it was very cold—"

"It was in the middle of winter."

"Then it had to be cold and I probably hated the long wait in the subway station and wanted to take a cab. But that's all I remember of that night—*all*. So now, after so many years, it seems silly for you to call me and worry about such a matter."

"I don't know. I'm sorry if I might have disturbed you with my call, but the matter seems important to me."

"Believe me it's silly. Because when you get right down to things, what's the difference about your old manuscript? From the way I knew Gabe then, and from what you and others have said about his condition since, he's much worse off than any of us now, published book or not. So forget whatever he might have done to you and just be thankful you have your health and also the time to write more."

"Maybe you're right. Take care, Pearl, and goodnight."

"No, be honest—I want you to answer me direct: am I right or not?"

"You are."

"Good. Speak to you soon."

Magna as the Good Woman

K ey's still in the lock, my hand still on the key when I'm grabbed from behind, his hand over my mouth same time he turns the doorknob, and pulls the key out, pushes me into the apartment and kicks the door shut.

"Don't scream or I'll kill you," he says.

Light's out. Normally I open the door, stick my hand past the jamb and turn the light on, first thing when I get home from school. So the room's dark, both his arms around me now, hand still over my mouth, my lips hurting from the pressure of his grip, shoulder bag he took from me and now holds, his mouth even closer to my ear.

"I mean it. Don't say a word. Do or try to get away from me or anything I don't want you to and I'll kill you. I've killed others. Women and men, I can kill you."

I shake my head. My hair brushes his face.

"What's that supposed to mean?"

He takes his hand away from my mouth a little. He could clap it back on in a second if I screamed. I'm not going to. I believe what he says. The way he grabbed and now holds me and way he speaks.

"I'll do what you say."

"That's a good woman. Now where's the rest of your money? Lead me to it."

He puts his hand back on my mouth and I start walking to the bedroom closet. I don't want to go to the bedroom with him but that's where the money is. If I said I didn't have any money he'd probably say I was lying. Everyone has some money at home. A ten, a five, and all of mine except for what's in the shoulder bag is in the closet in a box. Better to give it and maybe he'll get right out. So I start for the closet with him holding me from behind, arm around my chest, other hand on my mouth, my shoulder bag he's holding bouncing against my side.

"Don't turn the light on till I tell you," he says.

We're in the bedroom. He walks me to the window and pulls down the shade. Walks me to the light switch and says "Turn it on," and I turn on the light. Dumps what's in my shoulder bag onto the floor, takes the money from it and puts it in his pocket and kicks the bag and the books that came out of it across the room. "Now the rest of your money."

We go to the closet. He pulls the string and the closet light goes on. "I'm letting you go now only to get the money. Yell once and you are dead, dead," and he takes his arm from around me, pulls a knife out of his pocket, though the blade's still in the shaft. "You believe me, right?"

I nod.

"You can speak. I'm not preventing you."

"Yes."

"Yes what?"

"Yes 'sir'? What?"

"Do you believe what I'm saying?"

"I believe you, I believe you."

"You're not a beautiful girl."

"Thank you."

"I'm sure most men think you're gorgeous but to me you're ugly. And that's disappointing you are. Those are my odds though."

"What can I say."

"Get the money."

I reach up and get the shoe box off the closet shelf and give it to him. He opens it and takes the money.

"Anything else of value around?"

"I've a television, stereo, speakers, jewelry, mostly antique and costume. Take it all. It's all right."

"I know it's all right."

"I'm sorry. I was just saying."

"You're scared."

"Yes I'm scared."

"You smelled scared. Do I smell scared?"

"I don't know."

"Because I'm not. I'm happy. This was so easy. In getting into your downstairs was so easy and easier still that you gave me a safe place to stay for you on the stairs to the roof. You want men to wait for you to take all your things?"

"No."

"Sure you do."

"I don't. I've nothing to do with the design of the building. That was done fifty years ago and the old downstairs lock is the landlord's. Now please go. You have all my money."

"The jewelry, television, whatever else of value."

"I'm sorry, I forgot. Jewelry's in that case."

He grabs my arm and we go over to the jewelry case on the dresser. He opens it, looks it over, selects what he wants from it and sticks the jewelry into his pockets.

"That's the TV?"

"Only one."

"Too big. It'd take two of us to carry. Stereo's probably no good either. They'd see me a block away with it unless you have a suitcase I can fit it in. Where's the stereo?"

"The other room."

"I like this room."

"I don't have a stereo here."

"But I like it. A bed. Get undressed."

"Please, I don't want to."

"'Please, I don't want to.'" He takes the knife out of his pocket and opens it. "I've used this. But first show me the suitcase and stereo but suitcase first."

If I lived on the second floor I'd run to the window, throw it open and jump out and maybe even jump through it without opening it. I'd risk the stitches and broken leg, two of them, broken hips, a broken head, to avoid getting raped and maybe knifed and killed. But I'm four flights up. He'd beat me to the door. Or if I beat him to it, by the time I opened it he could knife me. Would he? How much is bluff? He seems he would. And knife me after he raped me? Seems there'd be less chance of that than his doing it if I tried to escape, just because I did what he asked and didn't anger him. I don't know. I'll give him what he wants, even suggest things I have he didn't think of—the blender, an antique figurine—and then plead with him to leave. If he doesn't, if he insists, if I see there's no way I can convince him otherwise or escape without getting knifed, I'll give in.

I get the suitcase out of the bedroom closet. He takes me to the livingroom, pulls down the shade, turns on the lights, says to sit right beside him on the floor next to the stereo.

"I don't think it'll fit," I say.

He turns it on, listens to it, unplugs and fits it into the suitcase by a couple of inches on all sides, closes the case and lifts it by the handle, testing its weight.

"It's so light I can even run with it."

"Now please go."

"First undress for me. Later I go."

"I don't want to undress. I want you to go. You got what you wanted. All this must sound trite. But you got what you wanted. You want a blender—a little valuable statue also, but the blender almost brand-new, take them. I'm not feeling well anyway."

"Blenders and toasters you get nothing for and statues can be traced. And you look fine."

"I've the flu. That's what my hacking's all about, maybe if not here then when I was coming upstairs. I'm also having my period. Besides that I've this terrible yeast infection down there that will end up in anybody's body—the genital area—that I come in contact with. It won't be worth it. You'll have to go to a doctor. It's quite crummy looking and will itch like mad for you when you get it. Just go. I won't report you."

"I'll see if you have infections and periods. Get undressed or I'll stick this in you now."

He puts the knife to my throat and motions me to stand. We stand and I take off my jacket and start taking off my blouse. He rips the blouse down when I get some of the buttons undone. He squeezes my nipples and steps back to observe them. "How come they don't get erect? Usually when I play with them like that they get erect. But I like a woman without a bra. Easy street door and roof stairs and no bunkmate or bra, you made it simple for me. Now the rest of you. Make it quick and I'll get out of here quick."

"Get out of here now. Please. I'm serious that I'm not well. And I swear I won't report you. But if you hurt me in any way I'll have to report you as I'll have to go to the hospital and they'll ask me and they'll call the police and I'll have to tell them about you. If they have your picture, I could recognize it without even wanting to."

"They don't have my picture. But if they did and even if I didn't hurt you, you'll go the police and look through a million pictures to find me. I've nothing to lose, whether I do anything more to you or not, that's what I'm saying, so take off the damn rest of your clothes."

I shut my eyes and just stand there. He pulls my belt out, unzips the skirt and pulls it down to the floor, pulls the panties down to my ankles, slaps my calf, I pick each of my feet up and step out of the panties and skirt and then he tugs on my sleeve and I take off what's left of the blouse.

"You're so hairy," he says. "Not that I'm complaining. You've nice legs and tits though. Turn halfway around." I do. "So-so. Now into the other room."

He sticks the knife into my arm and I feel the sharp end of it. I go into the bedroom with him beside me. He takes off his pants. He doesn't have on underpants. He's already erect. He motions me and I sit on the bed. He gets on the bed, lays the knife on the floor and says "Everything I want you do for me and don't even get a little mean." He grabs my head from behind and pushes it down till my cheek touches his penis and forces my mouth to the tip of it and says "Open your teeth and pull them back," and jerks my head up and down on it so I have to open my throat all the way or choke while at the same time he puts his finger in my vagina and says "Wet...get wet...I want to go in easy."

He does this with my head and his finger for a few minutes. At one point I start gagging and feel I have to vomit and he hears me and releases my head but not his finger.

"Don't throw up on me, I warn you. I'd kill you just for that."

"I won't."

"If I'm too big, I won't push you that far on me again—that's my one consolation."

"Okay."

What I'm feeling is I can't stand this. My eyes are shut when he brings me down on him again. I'm trying to imagine I'm someone else. Or that thing is something else but it can't be. Or I'm someplace else. Not with another man. At the moment I hate all men. I'm trying to think this isn't happening to me. I'm trying to think this can't be happening to me, it's a dream. And I'm a machine. Someone has turned me on, put a coin in the slot, put a plug in the socket, something, a battery in my head and me the machine I'm just performing as a machine would, top half of me going up and down on some other machine, doing a machine function but not with a man. I'm made of metal, solid, cold, disposable or with some crazy man, because my mind can't seem to change him into a machine, who likes doing it with a machine, but I can't feel it or him or even be thinking of that now because a machine can't feel or think.

But his finger's still in me and hurting my vagina. I don't want to get wet nor can I get wet at will. I try pulling out his finger. He keeps it in. I tap his hand holding my head. He keeps doing what he's been doing. I slap his hand. He lets go of my head and I sit up.

"I'm sorry. I didn't want to slap you but your finger's hurting me a lot. I told you I have a serious infection."

"You also said you were bleeding and have the flu."

"I do have the flu. I wasn't lying. And my bleeding stopped this morning but sometimes I can bleed more than a day after I think I've stopped. But the infection's real. I can't have sex. It's going to stay dry because of the infection. You're hurting me a lot down there, still hurting me, please let me alone and go."

He takes his finger out. "You're lying. And you have to have something. Every woman has something like Vaseline. Baby oil. Even regular cooking oil. Get any of those. Now which is it going to be?"

"I have some baby oil."

He goes with me to the bathroom, gets the baby oil out of the medicine chest and tells me to sit halfway off the seat and I do and he squirts oil into his palm and smears it in me. He grabs my wrist and leads me back to the bed. He shoves me into the bed. I'm on my back. I try to turn on my side but he slaps my chest and I stay on my back. He gets on top of me and sticks his penis next to my mouth.

"Open."

"Please."

He forces my lips apart by stretching the corners of my mouth till they hurt. He does the same thing he did before with my head. My neck aches this time and for the first time he's making groaning sounds. I look. He's staring straight down at me. I close my eyes. I wish he'd just come and then go. Maybe I should help him, jerk his penis a little to get it over with. I touch him there.

"No tricks. I want to do it fast but slow, my own speed. Hold it if you want."

I take my hand away. He does it the same way with me for minutes. My entire head hurts. I feel like choking but open my mouth wider so I won't. I can't get used to it or block it out. I even try to think he's someone I like doing it with, but nothing in my imagination works. I hate it, hate him. I want to bite him, kill him. I should do something. Biting him, he'd kill me or come close. Biting him off, I don't think I could do all the way through or even near to it and I have to do something I know for sure will incapacitate him completely and for minutes and that I know I also can do. Because I now think there's as much chance of him killing me as not. Before I thought there was more of a chance he'd just rape me and go. Now I think he'll rape me and then wait around taunting me and rape me again and maybe even a third time and then he'll hate me so much for having been raped by him or for whatever I am or have become to him or for any such reason that he'll kill me or knife me badly. Just to stop me from identifying him he could kill me. So I have to do something to him. All this while he's pushing my head back and forth on him and using his finger.

Then he stops both, takes a big breath, pulls on my earlobe almost tenderly and bends over and starts kissing me. Sticks his tongue in. He's very wet around the mouth.

His spit pours through, dribbles down his chin onto mine. He nips my lips with his teeth. Nips them harder and my tongue and I shriek and jerk my head away because he bit through my lip and I can taste my blood.

"I get overexcited," he says.

"Don't bite. You want to kiss, I'll kiss."

We start kissing. He puts his arms around me and I put mine around him and rub my hands up and down his back like he's doing to me. I want to get him involved with the kissing while I think of something to end all this. It takes a lot of concentration to kiss as if I mean it while same time trying to think hard about something to save my life. The knife. At the end of the bed on the floor. Not that I could get to it as he's much stronger than I and with one blow if I lunged for it he could knock me off the bed.

I could scream. He'll kill me. Fight back. Overpower me. Jab him in the eyes. I might not hit them right and then he could tie my hands up or something and I couldn't do anything more. His balls. I know they can hurt. I know how delicate they are for sure. Some of my men friends. Several times over the years I just touched their testicles a little more than a little and each one of them said it hurt. Don't even pat them one of them once said. One man's I just squeezed affectionately I thought and it gave him one of the worst jolts of anyone I ever saw. His stomach pain and being doubled up lasted half a minute or more and if a ball had hit it as happened a few times in his life, he said, he'd have dropped right to the floor. How in the service, he or another man said, one soldier was being strangled by another on top of him and when the top one wouldn't stop or get off, the bottom one smashed his testicles between his hand and the man on top was knocked unconscious by the blow and had to be hospitalized and almost died.

He stops kissing me. "Now spread your legs."

"Let me do it once more to you down there with my mouth."

"Don't tell me you're suddenly beginning to like it."

"As long as you're going to do it with me, I might as well enjoy it—I don't know."

"I don't believe that."

"It's the truth."

"The truth. Just lick it a little. I'll see how much you like it. You can be sure I'll get into it more if you do. Try anything funny though, you're finished."

"Lie back comfortably."

"I'm fine where I am."

He's sitting up. I bend over his penis and hold it with both hands and start to lick it. Then with one hand I stroke his testicles and then squeeze them real hard and he jumps and he's screaming but stops and starts coughing and choking and falls back on his back and bounces up and down on his shoulders and then I release them a little and shout "Don't move, stop bouncing, don't touch me, stay there or I'll squeeze them so hard they'll break and you'll die right here on the bed or else never move again—I know, I've worked in hospitals, so don't even try and get up, you hear? Say yes, say yes."

"Yes, yes."

I maneuver my knees to the floor while he's crying and saying "No, no, oh stop, please, oh," and I say "I'm going to let you go. But I'm first going to crawl you to the door while I squeeze your balls. I won't scream for anyone. I'll talk softly as I am now. You'll have to put up with the pain. I just want you out of here. You carry your pants while I crawl you to the door and put them on in the hall. What you do once you get out there is your business but I'll give you five minutes to get dressed and out of the building and then I call the police. That's a promise. But make one bad move, don't fool with me—try and hit me or get away, anything, whatever you try and do before you get to that outside hall and by the time your arm swings around or anything, I'll smash your balls in with my hands, okay?"

"Yes."

All this time I'm squeezing them just enough to keep plenty of pain coming in and he is in great pain. He's practically screaming. He probably would be screaming if he let himself make loud sounds. I say "Now turn around on the bed on your stomach and get off the bed backwards and slowly till you're on your knees in front of me and don't let me lose my grip on your balls. I'll be right behind holding on to them and you're to crawl very slowly to the door. I will kill your balls if you try anything but what I want you to, understand?"

"Yes."

He turns over on the bed and gets on his knees on the floor in the direction of the front door. I stand bent over behind him and keep squeezing them just so there's enough pressure to keep him in great pain. "Now move," I say, "crawl," and he starts crawling to the door while dragging his pants, all the time making noises how he hurts, "can't take it, go any more, the pain, oh, stop, please," hair and face full of sweat, tears coming out too. I don't say anything and it takes about five minutes to get to the front door.

I say "Now get up in a slight crouching position but with your rear end facing me." He does. I keep a tight grip on his balls with one hand and with the other unlock the door. "Now down," I say, "on your knees, rear end up," and I get on my knees too.

"Now I'm going to open the door by turning the doorknob and when the door's open enough for you to fit through, you start crawling through. When you're far enough out of the door I'll let go of you and slam the door, so bring in your foot or you'll lose that foot that's sticking out too."

"Neighbors."

"What about them?"

"See me. They. I'm caught."

"I'll look out first to see they're not there. I shouldn't be so kind to you."

"Have to. Or else. Else I try get you. Or away. But please, quick, hurry, no talk, to release me."

"Okay. Get in a crouch again. Rear up." He does and I stand, hold on to his balls with one hand and open the door. "Come closer to me." He moves towards me backwards. I can look down the hallway now. "Someone's coming up the stairs," and I duck back in and shut the door.

"Christ," he says. "Someone would. Let go. I won't run."

"No. You're a sonofabitch and I hate your guts and wish I could squeeze these to sawdust now but I can't because if I did you wouldn't keep your part of the bargain you're doing now, right?"

"Shh. They hear. I won't touch you. Too in pain. I'm. Can't even stand. Please. Let go. Killing me."

"Shut up. Step a step backwards." He does. I open the door, look down the hall. "Don't stop. Just crawl out slowly."

He starts crawling into the hallway. When his foot's just past the threshold I slam the door, lock and latch it and scream "Help, police, rapist, in the hallway, someone call the police, for the fifth floor, everybody call," when I really had thought I'd give him a few minutes to get away. I can't call as I want to be right here to snap the lock back if he somehow gets it unlocked or the latch back in or just to keep my shoulder against the door and myself screaming if he tries to get back in.

He doesn't. I look through the peephole and see him struggling to get his pants on. He's on the floor, having trouble getting the first trouser leg over the shoe. He's still crying, face in great pain. He stands with the pants, falls to the floor. He beats the floor with his fist, but lightly, as he doesn't seem to have the strength for anything more. I want to open the door and with the lamp near me smash him over the head. But he might suddenly revive by then. So I keep screaming and looking at him and his eyes are almost closed as he tries to get the same trouser leg over the shoe. Then he stands, holds his testicles and sort of drags himself with the pants in his hand to the stairs and down them.

Three days later I get a phone call. I'd seen the police here and went to the station and wasn't able to pick his picture out of the thousands they showed me. The man on the phone says "Remember me?"

"The police have a tap on all my phones."

"Bullshit. Think they can afford it every time some woman meets a new man? But you remember me."

"All right. Talk at your own risk. Longer the better I was told."

"You almost killed me with that hold."

"I wanted to, so feel lucky I let you go."

"You let me go because you had to. I wish I'd killed you when I had the chance from the start. I'm all better now. Took a couple of days to recover. You want to try it again?"

"Oh sure."

"I know your name."

"Get lost."

"Of course you don't and I wouldn't trust you if you said you did. You'd call the police and they'd be there in a minute. And that nutcracker grip of yours. Where'd you learn it? I want to know if it was in the newspapers before I met you and so how widespread it's known."

"Why the call?"

"You were a bastard for shouting like that when I was in the hall. You broke your promise."

"I didn't think. It was all my emotion unleashing or something. But you have to expect that when you treat someone as you did me."

"What did I do to you, Magna? Come on, just what did I do that's so bad to you?"

"You're so stupid. Anyway, you got away."

"You didn't see any photos of me at the police, did you?"

"No I didn't."

"There aren't any. But I have killed women. Nicer women than you too and I'm going to kill you. That's why I called. In the next week I'm going to get you on the street, force you into your apartment or a car or just be in your apartment or on the stairs again waiting for you. If you go to your friends I'll get you there and kill them too. First I'm going to rape you though till you hurt as much as you made me hurt. No more baby oil. I'm going to make you suffer real hard. And no chance of your hands stopping me because they'll be tied from the start."

"Finished?"

"No, I got much more to say."

"Well I don't." I hang up.

He calls right back. "I meant everything I said."

"Then I'll tell you what I mean and what I swear you made me be. If you ever come here or any place I am or whatever next time you say you'll try anything with me, I'll bite or slice but cut both your balls and your penis off—now take your choice, and you're right, I don't need any fucking police tap, but take your choice but that's what's going to happen to you, now do you hear me good?" There's silence at the other end and then he hangs up.

pp. 221-224

Page 221. I don't know if I can write it. It's taken me almost two years to get to this page. I don't have anything more to say. The novel's run flat. I don't want to go on with it. But after 221 pages? 220 I mean. And it's not true I don't want to go on with it. I do. I'm sure I can too, but I'm just bogged down. I have him where he's on a bridge. He has to make a decision about something. This has been the main point of the novel up till now. To have him go through the novel till the moment where he makes a decision that will change his life and also change the direction of the novel. I didn't know where he was going to make the decision. After the first hundred pages or so, it could have been almost anywhere in his journey through the city the novel takes place in. I didn't block out the novel from the beginning, just as I haven't with any of the novels I've written. But he should make the decision now. On page 221. There's no place else for him to go. It's late at night, he's alone on that bridge. Looking at the river about fifteen feet below. He knows he has to make the decision. He's been talking about it on and off through the entire novel. He left his apartment at dawn on page one to make the decision. A decision he knows will change his life. He hasn't revealed yet what the decision's about. Really hasn't revealed anything about the decision: just that he has to make one. What the decision's about is supposed to be revealed when he makes the decision. The reader's supposed to follow him around the city right up till the time when he makes the decision. I think I said that. Then he's supposed to make the decision. If he doesn't make it now there's nothing else he can do. He's done everything else in the novel but make that decision. At least everything else that would apply to his personality and life and actions and whatever other things apply, before he makes that decision. But what's the decision he has to make? He has to know what he has to decide on if he's to make the decision, and he has to make it. So make it. I'm telling him to make the decision. Say something out loud or in your head or even write it down if you want that will change your life and also change the direction of this novel. If those devices don't work, say it some other way. By a gesture or just one word or any way you think to say it, as long as it's clear to the reader that what you're doing is making that decision, but make it. If you don't, this novel's finished. It was all supposed to come to this. It has come to this. Right now there's no place else for you to go, nothing else for you to do but make that decision. So make it. I'm telling you to. Ordering you, damnit, I am ordering you to. The decision. Now.

Nothing comes. I wait. Nothing. No decision and nothing about the decision. I return to page 221 an hour later. Nothing comes. He doesn't move or say anything. He stays on the bridge. In the same spot, without a thought, gesture or word. Without doing anything, and everything around him stays the same too. I try to make something come to him or happen to him, so the novel could continue till the time he does make the decision, but nothing happens or comes. I return to page 221 a few hours later and do everything I can to make the decision come, to make anything happen around him or anything come, but nothing does. Then the next hour and then the next day. Each day after that, and many times a day some days, for two more weeks. Nothing.

I go to a bridge with the 220 pages, the same bridge I left him on, in the same city I've lived in for years and walked him through these last twenty to twenty-one months and throw the whole thing into the river. Most of the pages just sink. A couple of dozen or so float for a while downstream and sink. A few pages keep floating downstream till I can't see them. Four of the pages I threw float in the air till they land on the shore. One rolls into the river and sinks but the other three remain. No real problem. Nobody would know, if he found those pages, where they came from and probably not what they mean. Wouldn't really matter to me if anyone did. Wouldn't matter at all, in fact, not at all, and I mean that. I go home and sit down to start another novel, but with a new character for me. I'll make him older, of a different nationality, and with a wife. I'll put him in the country, since I've never written anything but about city life. I'll call him Bill or Phil or Ed, three names I've never used before. "p. 1" I write on the top left-hand corner of the page. Maybe that's as far as I'll get. I don't know, but I do care. "Bill walked into his house." So, there's more. I sit for hours and try to think of something to follow that sentence, but nothing comes that makes any sense. I get up and tell myself to come back to it later today.

Training to Magna

I t's been a long tough week of work and other things and for the train ride to New York I just want to be alone and rest. I walk the half mile from my apartment to the Baltimore station, buy my ticket and in the waiting room see every seat but one is filled. If I sit in it I'm almost sure someone on either side will start talking to me—it usually happens—so maybe I should just stand. But the train from Washington's been delayed by twenty minutes, the stationmaster says over the p.a. system, so I take the seat, put my overnight bag between my feet, my briefcase on my lap, close my eyes and think Just rest.

"When they say twenty minutes, do they mean thirty or even forty minutes?" the woman on my right side says.

"Talking to me, ma'am?"

"Yes, sorry, did I wake you? This is my first train trip, other than for that little subway under the Capitol in Washington, so I don't know if that announcement was only some delaying tactic for not telling us the train's going to be an hour late, possibly two."

"When they say twenty it usually means twenty and sometimes it means fifteen."

"You've ridden the trains from here a lot?"

"Every Thursday around this time," I say, "or really about three out of four weeks."

"You work in Baltimore and both travel that much?"

"I travel for personal reasons—to see a friend in New

York—but teach here."

"Community College?" the man on the other side of me says. "That's where my wife went nights."

"University of Maryland Baltimore County my school's called."

"Baltimore?" he says. "Oh yeah, I know the one. Way out in the sticks."

"Sort of, that's right."

"What do you think?" she says to him. "Our train from Washington will be an hour late, or only twenty minutes as the announcer and this man says?"

"Got me. I'm just stopping here. Seemed a good place to come in out of the rain."

"It's stopped," I say.

"Has? Well it had too one day, but I'll just sit a while more. For now I've no real place to go."

"When does the train reach Trenton?" she asks me.

"I'm not sure."

"Because you said you rode it so much, I thought—"

"This is The Montrealer. It's a slower train than I usually take."

"Which one's that?"

"The 5:15—I don't know the name. Excuse me. I just remembered something."

I go downstairs to the platform. There are two benches there. A man's sitting on the one nearest the stairs, so I go to the other. It's empty and I sit. I close my eyes.

"Mind if I sit here?" a man says.

"No no, of course." I look at my watch. I was asleep for two minutes.

"Your bags. I don't mean to, but if it's no problem?"

"Oh sorry, I wasn't thinking." I put the overnight bag on the ground and the briefcase on top of it.

"How far you going?"

"New York."

"Same here. I always wanted to catch the evening Montrealer. I like the club car idea. I don't like buying a split of wine and then sitting with it in my seat. I like the tables and chairs and, you know, to spread out a bag of peanuts or cards, even."

"It's much better," I say, "though there's usually too much smoke in there for me."

"Sure, I can see it if you don't smoke. You go up often?"

"Every now and then."

"I go twice a week. That's back and forth, back and forth two times. It gets boring but it's my work, and I wouldn't live there. Only way to liven the trip up is by taking the plane occasionally or getting different kinds of trains. The evening Montrealer is one I never got. The one in the morning from New York I've done a couple-dozen times, but it rarely carries the club car, don't ask me why, but if it does it's usually locked and they're only hauling it to Washington for this or some overnight Southern run. Besides, who wants wine at nine or ten in the morning—even eleven."

"You could have coffee. Or English muffins."

"You ever eat their English muffins, though the coffee's not bad."

"No, it isn't."

"It's not freeze-dried or instant at least. They make it in the pot."

"Yes, I've seen."

"You work here but also have business in New York?"

"I've a friend there, so occasionally I go for a long weekend."

"I'm out in Towson."

"That so?"

"Work there but live in Lutherville. Electronics. An Engineer, but now mostly supervision of sales. The Murke-

Mirablia Company."

"I don't know of it."

"One of Baltimore's largest employers. You'll see one of our warehouses on the way out."

The stationmaster announces our train. That means it'll be here in seven or eight minutes. "Excuse me," I say, and I get up, stretch, walk around the platform keeping my eyes on my briefcase and bag. People are coming downstairs, fanning out along the platform, a few heading with heavier luggage to the front where the sleeping cars will stop.

My feet hurt and I almost feel too tired to stand. So much preparing for classes this week, papers to read and grade, talking, talking in class and an inordinate amount of photocopying to do and departmental paperwork. And student readings. Two this week, and one visiting poet I had to meet at the airport, take to dinner, give the introduction for at her reading, go out for beers with after with some of the students, see her back to her hotel. And the old woman in my building. Three days in a row attending to this for her, that. Her lights blew because she overloaded one outlet. Next day she walked into my apartment two flights above hers. "Where am I?" she said. "I think I'm lost." That night she screamed up the stairs for help. I went down to her with the second-floor tenant, saw she was sick and called an ambulance and she said "One of you come with me to the hospital. They'll kill me if you don't," and I went with her, filled out her forms and helped take her to her room. Then called the landlord and said "Don't you know if she has somebody?" and he said "You don't think I want her out also, but so long as she doesn't want to she doesn't have to go to a home," and next day calling the twenty people with her last name in the phonebook.

I go back to the bench. "Almost here," the man says. "You can see the locomotive's light on the rails. Another reason I

prefer The Montrealer is it's much roomier inside. And
window curtains. You laugh, but if you want to sleep all you
have to do is draw the curtain, put your legs up on the leg rest
and conk out. In the morning the curtains are only useful
against the sun if you sit on the left side of the train going
south. Which side would that be? I should know. I'm the
engineer. The left side would be, well—heading south—let's
see. My left hand. I'm going south." He holds out his left
hand, faces the direction the train's coming from. "South,"
he says. "I'm going south. It would have to be east, of course,
the left side, wouldn't it?"

"I think so."

"I don't know why it's suddenly so confusing. But we'll
say east. I must have a block about it. It has to be east, that's
right. All that water from the Susquehanna and Chesa-
peake we pass pouring into the inlet. The tankers docked in
Wilmington. And God help me, the sun rises there also. So
the curtains are only useful on the east side in the morning,
but I usually sit—"

"There's the train."

"Great," and he picks up his valise. I hold my bag and
briefcase. The train stops. Lots of people are around us now.
We stand to the side of the door as the conductor and
passengers come out.

"Which one's the nonsmoking?" I ask the conductor.

"Rear car and one to your left."

I go to the door on my left. The man's right behind me. I
go in and he says "I smoke, but don't have to—I've in fact
been warned not to, so if you want to continue our conversation?"

"I have to go much farther—something about the backs
of trains."

"You can't go too much farther and you're not that far
back. Next one's probably a smoking car and then the club

car and after that the dining car they won't let you into till about eight."

"I'll try. Nice talking to you." I walk through the car, turn around at the end of it and see him putting his valise on the luggage rack. He sees me and points to the seats under the rack. I shake my head, point to the next car and tap the door-opening device.

I don't want to sit in the smoking car so I go into the club car. There don't seem to be too many smokers at the tables. I get a beer from the service bar, sit at an empty table, give the trainman my ticket and get back a seat check.

"Mr. Taub," a young man says. I look up. I don't recognize him. Dark sunglasses, bangs almost over his eyes.

"Ed Shekian. I was in Ida's class last term."

"Ida?" I'm sitting and he's standing.

"Ida Rulowitz. She invited you to speak to us because you're the expert in I don't know what. Robert Frost, I think."

"Wallace Stevens?"

"That's right, Stevens, Pound and Eliot. You said you knew more about Stevens' work than Pound or Eliot, but that you maybe knew enough of their work for our class. It was an introduction to contemporary lit. Well, I saw you running up the aisle past me before and I thought 'Whew, Mr. Taub, there he goes, I got to get him,' so I just dumped my stuff on a seat and ran after you. You remember Ida. How is she, you know?"

"Oh sure, Ida. She had an awful accident."

"A woman on a motorcycle with about ten hours experience on it and on a major highway and without a crash helmet no less. That is just stupid, as smart a teacher and nice a person as she is."

"Yeah, god, awful. Someone told me about her only last week. I didn't know. The school's so big. She was supposed to be getting out of intensive care this week, this person said."

"I knew that. I thought you might've known more. I wanted to visit her but they said not yet. Her boyfriend did. Look, excuse me for presenting this to you like this, but remember you said you'd do a radio interview for us?"

"For you? Did I? In what way?"

"For the campus radio station. You see, this year I've even a bigger position than I had last year. Not only chief engineer but the program coordinator too, and I'm trying to boost the programs on literary content a notch. You said, when a few of us talked to you after class, that you'd let yourself be interviewed in a Q and A session and maybe then would read some contemporary poems you like. Would you still be interested?"

"I don't know. I don't like to be on programs or even panels. I'm not asked that much, granted, but the microphone and I aren't great friends."

"Oh, I've seen you introduce poets here. You do a terrific job. And we loved you in Ida's class. Most of us thought that could've been the best one all semester."

"I still don't know. Listen, why don't you sit? You want a beer? I'm having one."

"Sure, why not, this is great. I love meeting teachers like you who are famous on their own and also are great teachers and just talking with them casually like this. I'll be right back."

"You have enough money?"

"Why wouldn't I? You mean for the beer?"

"Since I invited you, and I make more than enough, which partly comes from your tuition. And you must be paying—are you an out-of-town student?"

"From Staten Island. It costs a fortune, but I help out with three thousand of it. My father said—well it wasn't even that. I just think it's what I should do, contribute to my education monetarily."

"Three thousand's a lot though."

"I work as a mason in the summer. Not a full mason but a step above apprentice. The mason I work under—"

"Why don't you get your beer?"

"Right. Your neck must be hurting, looking at me turned around."

He gets a beer, comes back, sits opposite me. He tells me why he chose our university, what he thinks of sharing an apartment with three men, the premed courses he's not doing very well in, his mother who was terminally ill for three years and which made him choose medicine as a career. His father and younger brothers: "They're going to be so surprised when I walk in the door."

"Maybe you should call them from the station. People today get alarmed when the door opens and you don't expect anyone."

"No, they like surprises from me. Just like my girl will too."

"Now she you definitely should have told you were coming. You know, I'm not saying anything, but you don't want to set yourself up for being embarrassed or hurt."

"She's okay. I'll show up tomorrow early. She lives with her folks."

"I'm sure you're right." I yawn. "Sorry—just a little sleepy. It's been a hectic week. But go on."

We're pulling into Aberdeen. We must have been speaking half an hour. He's talking about the fifty hours a week he works at the campus radio station. "I do it because I love it. I'd have to—I don't get paid." About the difference of being a freshman and sophomore. Ida and her accident. Some of the interesting people he's met here: teachers, students. The time he barged into the university president's office to get more money for the station. I'm yawning again. "Did you really?" I say. The train pulls out of Wilmington. My glass is empty. I don't know whether to excuse myself and go back to the nonsmoking car or stay here. I don't want to hurt his feelings. I do want to get some rest. Oh, put up with it a little more. Best way is with another beer.

"I'm going to have another," I say, standing up. "Can I get you one?"

"Sure, why not? No, I probably shouldn't. Two with no food in me makes me high."

"Then you better not. I forgot how old you are you speak so well. That's not a put-down either. You're very articulate and mature and have done a lot of things with your life. Then I'm going to go in back now, if you don't mind, and find a seat."

"Me too, though I already have one, or my bags do. Say, maybe there's a seat available next to mine. There was when I followed you in here. Whoops, I shouldn't have said that again, right? Sounds like hero worship, which it's not. I just think you're an incredibly nice smart guy."

"Thank you."

We start back, I first. Coming toward me in the smoking car is the man I spoke to on the platform. I move to the side so he can pass. "How you doing?" I say.

"Hey there," he says. "I'm about to check out the dining car if they let me see it. They're not all the same on The Montrealer. Where'd you finally find a seat?"

"Haven't got one yet."

"My car's filled. They should lose some seats in Philadelphia but maybe take as many on. If I see you later in the club car, let's continue our chat."

"This is a student at my school. Ed—and I don't know your name."

"What, you teach? I did too. U of P. Five years. Engineering."

"That's what I thought of taking once," Ed says.

"Tickets, please," the trainman says.

We each show him our checks.

"So I'll see you," I say to the man. I go through the smoking car. A few vacant seats. Maybe there'll be a couple of vacant ones in the nonsmoking car, no matter what the man said.

"I guess you're in the next one too," I say to Ed.

"Second aisle by the door."

We enter the nonsmoking car. Seat next to Ed's is taken. "Maybe I can get her to move," he says.

"No, it wouldn't be fair. Speak to you later perhaps."

I go further up the aisle. There's a vacant seat before and after the one that man had put his valise above. I don't want him to see me when he gets back, nor do I want to speak to Ed anymore, so I go through the next smoking car into the rear nonsmoking car and look for a seat. They're all occupied or have seat checks above the seat or something on the seat if nobody's sitting on it. I return to Ed's car, choose the aisle seat in the third to last row and put my overnight bag on the luggage rack. The man next to me smiles at me when I sit, then continues looking out the window. He has no newspaper or book around him, so I'm afraid he's going to be another one who will ultimately want to talk to pass the time. I turn on my reading light, take out a book from my briefcase. My check, I think, and I take the check out of my shirt pocket and stick it in the holder above the seat. It comes loose and drops on the floor by the man's foot. "Excuse me," I say, bending down to get the check.

"Yoach a pono," he says. "Yoach a pono—no."

"Uh...what?"

"Anglish. No English. No speak. No American." He puts his fingers over his closed lips, hunches his shoulders as if to say he's sorry.

"Really, it's okay," I say. "Really. No problem."

He smiles and turns back to the window. I put the check into the holder and my book back into the briefcase and turn off the light. I look behind me, am about to tell the woman in that seat that I'm about to move my seat all the way back so I can sleep, so if she has a drink on the seat tray, hold on to it, then think Don't say anything, don't start. I press the seat button and very slowly let the seat all the way back. I rest my head on the seat's side rest and close my eyes.

"Hey, how are you?" the man from the platform says. I keep my eyes closed, pretend not to hear. "Oh, sorry. Must be asleep."

"Mr. Taub," Ed says about twenty minutes later. "There's a seat next to mine now."

"Shh," the man I'm sitting beside says. "Shh shh shh."

Finished

I can't finish anything anymore. I try but can't. I spend most of my night working. Then I take a short nap and go to my paying job and work all day there and come home and have a quick bite and sleep for a few hours and wash up and go to my desk, but much as I work there, nothing gets finished. I try to finish. I try extra hard. I've been working harder at my work and at trying to finish something these last few months than I have in twenty years. Sometimes I work eight hours straight, time off to walk around the room, do some exercises, have a snack, go to the bathroom, time off for all that. Then back to my desk and I work eight hours, ten hours, but never straight. Three hours of actual straight work at the most, perhaps. Maybe four. Of just sitting down and doing it without getting up, I mean. Then time off for a snack, to relax with a brief walk around the room, to get the kinks out with some hard physical exercise in the room, maybe even to sit on the couch and drink coffee and read a newspaper for about fifteen minutes, newspaper which I bought when I went to my paying job earlier that day. And a couple of times in the last few weeks, time off to go outside and around the corner to the all-night grocery for a quart of milk, pound of coffee, bread. Just a few items as I don't want to waste much time buying or preparing or cooking foods, time I could be spending on my work. Maybe also some sandwich meat and sliced cheese and a jar of mustard or mayonnaise if I'm out of it so

73

I'll have something easy to snack on when I work at home and something to smear on the snack so it won't be so dry. Then back to my desk where I'll continue my work but never finish any of it. I've boxes filled with things I can't finish. Ream boxes, not big carton boxes, and the city dump must have buried or burned another twenty pounds or so of my work that I haven't finished these last few months.

When I first started doing this work at home I used to finish all of it. Ninety-five percent, ninety-eight, so just about all. Then I'd finish a little less—after doing this kind of work for about ten years—but not much less. I wouldn't be able to finish about ten to fifteen percent after about ten years of this work at my desk. Five years after that, and still putting in five to six hours a day every weekday at it and maybe eight to ten hours a day on free weekends and vacations, I couldn't finish at the most twenty-five to thirty percent of what I started. But never any more than that, and those last figures might even be too high by about five to ten percent. But now, after twenty years at it—twenty-five, counting what I called then my self-apprenticeship, when it didn't matter if I finished what I started or not; I was just teaching myself to start then, teaching myself to continue and finish—well, after twenty years at it I can't finish anything. This has been going on—but I already said for how long. Months. If I said a few, I was either intentionally misleading myself or just wrong. It's been eight months, nine. Before that I wasn't able to finish about eighty percent, but still, I finished twenty percent and thought, with all the work I did, that that was enough. That twenty percent was almost a distillate, if that's the right word—a refinement— but distillate's close enough. I don't want to get bogged down now over this word or that and end up where I can't finish this piece too. I want to finish it because maybe with a finished piece I'll have started something and I'll be able to finish a piece right after this one and maybe all the pieces or just about all of them right after this one I'll be able to finish if I finish this one, till I'm finishing as much work as I used to finish when I first started this kind of work after I felt I'd served enough time at my self-apprenticeship. Maybe this piece will start something like that. It feels like it. Feels as if I'm going to finish this piece. That's what it certainly feels like.

But where was I? That's more important. Because if I don't finish this, then I wouldn't have started anything going but this piece. I have to get back where I left off and finish that line or thought and then come to a finish in this entire piece. I was saying something about a distillate. Not that part that that word was close enough. That—that's right—and don't get off the subject anymore or you'll never get back to that lost line or thought—that the twenty percent I finished a year or so ago was perhaps a distillate of the work I started—I think that was it—sure—and so finishing twenty percent of what I started was enough to make me feel that my work was going along okay. All right, that might not have made the sense I intended it to—started out to do—might not have been what I started out to say in that thought about the distillation of my work—but it's enough. I can't expect everything all at once if I'm going to get back to finishing my first piece in eight to nine months. Just to finish this one, that would or should be enough. It would be, and what I just said, well, something of what I intended to say must have got through. But where was I again? It was enough; finishing twenty percent was; eight to nine months ago and more. But now I can't finish anything. No distillates. Not even one percent. If it was one percent I finished of all the work I started, would that be enough? Yes, anything—I'll say yes to anything, I mean, just to finish this piece. So yes it would, yes it would. Because if I do finish this, well, I already said what I thought would happen. What was that? Just to remind myself what it was. Because I forgot. Maybe that's my problem. Not only digression but forgetting what I start out to say. That's perhaps why I can't finish anything. Is that it? What? That I forget. Forget what? Now you're just joking. No I'm not. What was I saying just now? Something about distillates. No, that was before. Then what? Something about twenty percent. One percent. That if I finish one percent, it wouldn't be enough. I don't think I said "wouldn't" then, but it's what I think now. Why? Well, it's just not enough. Even to get started in finishing pieces? Yes. After all, think of all the work that went into that one percent. Ninety-nine percent work. Or rather, a hundred percent work, one percent finished. Is that right? I'm not sure. Figure it out mathematically. I'm not good with numbers. But it's a simple problem. One from a hundred is ninety-nine. Still. Then what? What what? Let's see, where was I? Something about work. No, that was from somewhere far off. Another piece perhaps. Even three pieces back, maybe four. Give it up. Maybe that's the best idea yet.

Magna Out of Earshot

She calls and says "I just heard. It's terrific news. Lilly just phoned and told me. I can't tell you how happy I am."

"Yes, I told Lilly a few days ago. I didn't know if she'd tell you."

"It's just wonderful. That you could do it, and so easily. And she's met the woman. She says she's so intelligent and nice. I'm so happy. I know it's what you wanted. I wish it would've worked for us as easily. After three years with her, and—well, it's just beautiful. Five years with me and we still couldn't do it, right? It was always bad timing, always that bad timing, that's what did it. I'm sorry. But I'm glad it's now going to finally happen for you."

"Yes. Thank you."

"What you always wanted. Maybe we should've married. You wanted to so much—and the baby. You wanted that so much too. I didn't. I couldn't—it was absolutely the wrong time. Do I repeat myself too much?—but it was. You don't want to have a baby when all you're thinking about is breaking apart, right? And getting rid of the baby—well, not a baby, but it would've been much more than a baby by now—that was the real killer. But I'm so happy for you. Ecstatic, really. When's it going to happen?"

"The marriage?"

"The marriage, the wedding—of course, what else?"

"We think around February. February 8th to be exact. A

very small wedding. Just my brother and sisters and their spouses and my mom and Magna's parents and her uncle and aunts."

"Magna, that's right."

"Maybe her closest friend too—someone who was like a sister to her and still is—but that's it."

"Magna. I like it. It's a great name. Sounds European, though that's not why I'm saying I like it."

"Her parents came from there. She was born here."

"Well, that should make her a little closer to you and your family, with your background, and also the same religion Lilly says. That's probably wise, not that we ever had any trouble that way. But I'm so happy for you. It's just fantastic. I know I'm overdosing with the gushes here, but you don't know how happy I am for you. I know how much marriage means to you. How much you wanted to marry me. At times I wanted to marry you too. Now I don't think it'll ever happen with me again—marriage. I've been in love all of four times, married once, I'm 41 and my last big love affair was with you which started when I was 32."

"Don't worry, it'll happen again."

"That's nice of you to say, but I don't think so. But I'm so glad she's such a nice person. She must be a bit wild too, right? Because if I know us both, we couldn't have anyone who wasn't just a little wild. That's what I think and there are so few wonderful and comfortably wild people around. But what are your plans after the wedding?"

"For her to continue teaching in New York, me in Baltimore, and then in May, when her contract ends—well, even if it didn't, since my job is much better than hers—to get a two-bedroom apartment here and for her to move in with me. For us to move in together, I mean."

"That's wonderful. And you don't know how much I appreciate, and Lilly does, your including her in your wedding plans. She says you invited her to it, but her winter break will be over by then, so before she goes you're having a pre-nuptial party at Magna's place for Lilly and your nieces and nephews."

"We didn't want—couldn't have, really, all of them at the wedding. Lilly, yes, because, well, since I lived with you both, she's a little more special than the rest. Maybe that would've been wrong, having her at the wedding and not the others—I'm not sure."

"No, it's wonderful and right. You've been like a second father to her. In some ways, better for her than her father. Oh, maybe you just balance him out. But I'm so lonely without her. What a change. For both of us—maybe you too. The place seems so empty. At first I'd come home and call out for her. 'Lilly, Lilly.' Nicky thought I was crazy."

"Nicky?"

"Your 'Licky Nicky'—the cat. I also called home a couple of times and wondered why there was no answer. Nuts, right? Why isn't she home from high school? I thought. High school? She's in college—in California—and has a serious love interest going."

"No."

"Yes. Don't be upset."

"I'm not. She's just too young."

"She's not too young. She might even be a year or two behind. I'm not pushing her, of course, but I can't be a hypocrite. I was doing it at sixteen. And by serious, I don't know about how serious. It could still be innocent—a little hand holding, a kiss. I will be meeting him at Thanksgiving, though. I'll be out there on business and arranged to stay a few extra days and Lilly says we're having dinner at his apartment. He's cooking it all himself, trimmings included."

"He must be pretty capable then."

"He's nice, she says, and one of their brightest students,

and I just love it that you react to it like her real father. It shows how much she means to you. And she's really only a phone call away from us, right? So I've adjusted to it, but I still hate to be home alone. Hate it, but nothing I can do."

"Come on, that won't last long. You're intelligent and attractive and very successful now for someone who changed her profession such a short time ago. You'll meet someone. Some guy in your field, for instance, in New York, or when you do make these trips."

"God no. They're all in vests. But tight vests, each trying to outdo the other to look like a high-powered exec, and they only read books and listen to music and look at art for entertainment. They tell me this. To my face. I think, Jesus, boy, they sure don't know me. Oh, I got interested in a couple of them the last year, but after a month they get so damn boring. That's what I mean about being a little wild. Not crazy, just loose. These men don't say or do anything but what's relevant to their profession or what you and I would never get seriously interested in. Football. Can you believe it? Picture me at a game—one guy took me to one. 'Rah rah' he wanted me to say. They think it's unusual I don't know anything about it—or cute, that's the word one used, and he's going to teach me. I'll tell you. When I look around, and hear the same complaints from a dozen other intelligent attractive women, I realize what I had in you."

"Gee, that's—"

"No no, that's no slight. You certainly weren't perfect— I wasn't in any way either—but at least you were devoted and faithful, a bit tortured sometimes, but you would have been okay. You would have been very nice to come home to after work. You were always sweet and concerned or mostly always. You cooked. You were clean. You had some humor and were a lot deeper and not pretentious and cold like these men. I suppose I should have stayed with you, but that awful bad timing always messed it up, right? It killed us. I was just coming out of a bad ten-year marriage, you were coming out of about five years of complete loneliness. All wrong. Too bad. Because I wish it had worked. It would have if I had let it I suppose. But I couldn't have, so it's not as if I mind now. And I'm thrilled the way it worked out for you. You're happy now, and you have what you always said you wanted most."

"In my personal life, yes—I'm very happy. She's very nice."

"She must be. You wouldn't choose anyone else but someone extremely bright and wonderful, and someone like that would only choose someone like you."

"Thanks, but that's not quite exact. If anyone, you know that. I've been impossible with some women and some haven't been too easy on me. I don't mean you. That was something different."

"How so?"

"Well, I mean, I was with you longer than with anyone I've known, and I was really in love with you and it was really reciprocated, so we had everything: good, great, indifferent and bad."

"That's what I meant, really. That when you finally choose someone permanent, it'd be, and same with her, like the way I said."

"Then I guess I'd agree."

"Terrific. We got that settled. So, and not because this is long distance—I've a company card for that—it's been nice talking to you, Will. It's actually been great. It made my day, when Lilly told me the news. Married, she said—can I believe it? Nobody—at your age—thought you ever would. And she loves Magna. Pretty and gentle and intelligent, etcetera, she said about her. I love it. Love everything about it. That you've been so kind and attentive to Lilly since we broke up I love most of all. You changed her way of looking at men, probably forever. She'll know that one day. You did it by continuing to see her and love her as a friend, rather than till you stopped living with us, and putting her in your plans. That they have—men do—this other side to them—the female side—or can have it—or maybe they always do, but you just didn't suppress it—so you made her see them as more complete people and with a stabler eye. That doesn't make sense. As stabler, thoughtful, gentle creatures I mean, and rounder, more complete. I mean—oh—I love you. Marry me."

"Uh, what?"

"Oh Jesus, I said it. 'I love you. Marry me.' I said it. But I mean it. This week. And you heard me. Don't make it worse for me—harder. Do you think you can do it? Because I swear, I swear, it'll work out. I'll give you a child."

"Now wait wait wait—"

"I'm older than Magna but I can still have a child. I've been tested, and I want one more in the worst way. I'll be a great mother. You've seen me be one. And I'll be much better with you than I was even in our best moments. I'll honor us always."

"Linda—hold on—listen to me."

"A loving wife. I mean, within reason of course. Meaning, if we love one another it'll be as near to perfect as a marriage can be. I'll see to it. I'll work as hard as I ever worked on anything for that. And I'd never forget what you were giving up, nor ever gloat over it. So marry me. Run away with me even. Tonight even. I mean it. Could you? Will you? And I'm not pulling your leg. And running away isn't—aren't the words I want to use. I can fly or train to Baltimore or you can come to New York, and if not tonight then sometime this week."

"No I can't. Thank you though for asking. Listen, how do I answer this?—but it wouldn't be right. And I am—I'm very satisfied with Magna. Honestly."

"Too bad. I just thought—well, just too bad. I gave it a shot. I wanted it to. It was on my mind. I still do. I'd still love for you to say yes, you'll marry me. You know everything could be good. I'd be everything to you, which isn't to say Magna isn't now. And what else? Just that I love you, and it's not just some craziness in my head that I do, and I can't bear to think I'm going to be alone."

"You won't be for long. You're really wonderful—truly so. You have everything."

"I'm 41."

"And I'm 46. And a man, so the age difference, I know—but so what? But whatever. I can't. You understand. And if I'm flubbing in what I'm trying to say, it's not my fault. I love you and did then when we were together as much as I love Magna now. I mean I love her as much now as I loved you then, and I still think the world of you. But Magna and I are working—together, we're just together, very close—you know, and getting married."

"Of course. I just thought you might go for it. No, that sounds too flippant. I just meant it, period. And if you had gone for it, I would have done whatever you wanted. Given up my job. I still would if you'd go for it. I'd go wherever you wanted. That's a lot different an attitude than I had before."

"It is, but please. We'll get together when Lilly comes in. She is coming around Christmas time you said. She said so too."

"Yes. That'll be nice. We'll have dinner. You're not mad at me that I asked?"

"No. But it's—well, you know."

"It's something you might have done, but about ten years ago, right?"

"Six, seven even. I guess. Yes. It is. Maybe."

"Oh, I could kick myself that we didn't work out. For all

I know, maybe the timing wasn't as bad as I thought then and as you said it wasn't. I can be such a fool."

"No, you were terrific then. I loved you and all that and you were right. It wasn't the right time. It never would have worked."

"Then why'd you think it would?"

"I was wrong."

"When I got pregnant it would have. You wanted the baby so much. I should have had it. First of all, it would have been closer in age to Lilly and safer to deliver. And after a year, I still would have been able to do what I've done by now, or maybe just be a year behind. I can kick myself, kick myself. You were such a lovey about it. Terrible about other things sometimes, but never horrible. Just temperamental, but you would have become what you are now, mellowed, and maybe even quicker than it took you without the baby and me. And combining that with your overall loveiness, it would have been perfect. I'm sure of it."

"Probably. I'm sorry. And I'm still fairly terrible at times. Honestly, it isn't so easy for Magna, though it is easier than it was for you. It'll be the same for you with someone else. Next man you land—that'll be the best one."

"I hope you're right. But one more last chance? You won't run away with me? I won't ask you again."

"Wish I could but I can't."

"Now you're being just cutesy."

"Then no, I really can't, Linda. I'm getting married in two months, but your offer was certainly attractive."

"Now you're being charming."

"Then I just can't—what do you want me to say?—I just can't. I love Magna too much. And I can't just drop her—what the hell you think I am? And we want to have a kid. We want to do a lot of things. I'm deeply, deeply in love with her, and your invitation, if I'm supposed to take it seriously, is plain ridiculous, did you know? And if I'm not supposed to take it seriously, well, I don't know. It's either silly or not thought out or maybe even vindictive, but it's something that sure the hell surprises me coming from you."

"Now you're being too honest. But that's the best of the bunch I guess. You know..."

"What? Really what? Because actually, I have a—"

"Don't talk about work you have to do now."

"Okay, I won't. What is it you were going to say?"

"I really did think there might have been a chance."

"Then you're saying you were serious? Because if you were, then I apologize."

"I was, very much so. It was a long shot, but a chance. You rat. Because now, finally, you'd be happy with me."

"Please, no more?"

"Very happy—believe me you would. Me too. Oh, you'd feel horrible about her for a while, but you'd eventually get over it. Because you're still in love with me somewhat— admit it—and that would be enough to start on. Or actually don't. Say you're not if you want."

"I'm not, really. I think about you a little and dream about you more than I have in years, but I'm not quite sure what that all means. Maybe I'm anxious—you know, that I don't want to happen with Magna what happened with you, because if it did I'd think that'd be the end of ever having a close relationship with a woman—so that's coming up. Because the situations in some ways are the same. Being with one person so long, thinking about having a baby, possibility of marriage, and so on. But in that special way, I'm now only in love with Magna. Now that's the truth. I swear it."

"I believe you believe it, but just a little of me says you feel you have to believe it. Anyway, goodnight, you lucky dog. And forget about dinner together with Lilly—that would be impossible now. If you want to see her, arrange it for yourself. In fact, this should probably be the last time we speak to each other for a long while, unless there's something important—even borrowing my car if you really need it—that I can do for either of you in some way." She hangs up.

Will the Writer

He calls up a bookstore and says "Do you have a book by the name of *Forewarned* by William Taub?" The man who answers says "Who's the publisher?" and Will tells him and the man says "Just a second." He goes, comes back and says "No, we haven't got it but I can order it for you," and Will says "I need a copy right away as a present, but thanks."

He calls another bookstore and says "Do you have a book called *Forewarned* by someone named Taub or something—I suppose that's his last name. The publisher is South Street Press." The woman who answers says "Fiction, nonfiction?" and he says "Fiction—a novel or collection of novellas I think. Anyway, one of those, and in hardcover." She says "I never know what we have around here, let me check," and goes, comes back and says "His name's William Taub, it's a novel, and we don't have it. Like me to get a copy for you?" and he says "No thanks—I don't need it immediately. I'll drop by in a few days and if there's a copy there, I'll buy it then."

He calls another bookstore and says "Do you have the newest novel by William Taub? Though maybe he goes by William E. Taub as he did with his first novel, but I guess it doesn't make a difference." "What's the book's title?" and he says "I don't know but thought you might if I just gave you his name. I know the book's out though, from a South Street Press—maybe a month ago, maybe a month and a half. You have a way of looking up the title if you have the author's name?" and she says "In a supplementary publication called *Forthcoming Books* if it's not in the main one *Books in Print.* Can you hold on?" She comes back and says *"Forewarned—* that should be the one. Are you interested in buying it?" "Yes, do you have it?" and she says "No, but we could special-order it, which would mean an additional charge of fifty cents. It's from a fast distributor, so should be here by tomorrow or the day after at the latest." "I'll be in," he says and she says "What's your name so I can put it aside for you?" "Oh, I'll be in, don't worry," and hangs up.

He calls another bookstore and says "There's a new book I was asked to get—*Foreshadowed* or *Forearmed* or something like that—I know it has a fore with the hyphen at the beginning of the one-word title and an e-d at the end. I'm afraid I'm going to make it a little tough for you today, because I also don't have the author's name or his or her publisher." *"Forearmed?"* the woman says. *"Foreshadowed?* Doesn't strike anything familiar. Maybe someone else here has heard of it." She says away from the phone "You know of a new book, no author or publisher given, called *Forearmed* or *Foreshadowed* or *Fore-* something else perhaps?" The person she speaks to says something and she gets back on the phone and says "Could it be by William or Warren Taub and the publisher South Street Press? The manager here says she remembers from their catalogue or their salesman's sales pitch a book with a title close to that by an author with a name similar to one of the ones I gave you." "I don't know. I was told it's a novel—I forgot to tell you that— and to pick it up for a friend, but that's all." "Well, if it's here—no, the manager just waved to me we don't have it— she went through both the new fiction and nonfiction shelves. If you want I could get it for you in a few days." "Maybe I'll try another store first, because this person really wanted the book quickly, and if let's say two more don't have it I'll call back and order it from you."

He calls another bookstore and says "Do you have a book by W. E. Taub? I don't know if that's a woman or a man—I assume it's a woman because of the initials—but the title is something like *Forenoon* or *Foretaste*. Maybe the last one can't be it. Anyway, it's a novel, or collection of stories, but fiction, and new, and the publisher I'm sure is South Street Press, not one I've heard of but maybe you have." "Oh yes," the man says, "—a very good publisher." "Good. Anyway, it just came out, this book, and because of its theme, which apparently applies to what I'm working on now, or at least this person who told me about it thought so, I was told to get it." "I do remember seeing something written up in one of the publishing weeklies, I think, about a book called *Forewarned*—could that be the one?" "*Forewarned*. Yes, that's it—you have it?" "Let me check." He comes back. "We don't have it. I could easily put in an order for a copy—even send it to you if you have an account here or if you want to pay for it through a credit card and it's one we honor." "I don't have an account with you and I let my credit card lapse. Can you do me one more favor and tell me the price of the book and if W. E. Taub is the author's right name?" "I'd have to look that up." Will says nothing. "This might take a couple of minutes," and he goes, comes back, says "It's William Taub. And sixteen ninety-five, for a hardbound, which isn't bad for today. Probably around a hundred-sixty to a hundred-eighty pages." "But you don't have it in stock," and the man says "If we did, believe me there's no reason I'd hold it back from you." "That's really too bad. You see, I've tried around and every bookstore seems to know of the book and says there's been a demand for it—or at least some people have asked about it—but no store so far has it. You've any idea why that is?" "Perhaps they're all just about to receive it after having put orders in some time ago. Or else they had copies and they all recently ran out of them because of some television or print coverage of the book or a major book review or some kind of publicity, though I'm unaware of anything like that." "Maybe South Street's a particularly slow publisher in getting its books to the stores." "Not from my experiences with them, but I do know we haven't ordered any copies of this book. It would be on this list I have in front of me now. One more thing. If you do order from us, you'll have to come in and pre-pay by cash or send us a money order for the exact amount." "I could do that myself through the publisher, couldn't I?" and the man says "I suppose so, but it'll take two weeks to a month longer to get it that way. And by ordering direct from the publisher you'll also have to pay the mailing costs of a dollar or more. But do what you want, sir, please."

He calls another bookstore and says "I was in last week for a new book by William Taub, called *Forewarned*, from South Street Press. You didn't have a copy then, so I wondered if you might have got it in by now." "Did you speak to me about it," the woman says, "because sometimes the books come in and they're not on the shelves yet." "No, I didn't speak to anyone. I just looked, didn't see, and left." "Let me see if we have it," and she yells out "Henrietta, check if *Forewarned* by Taub in the—what category is it?" she asks Will. "Fiction, reference, history?" and he says "A novel. Thin. About two hundred pages. With a painting on the cover by Anselm Morand of an empty white room—maybe you know of it—empty except for two easy chairs, which have a just-sat-in look, and a lit fireplace in it." "No, I don't know that one by Morand. —In the fiction section," she yells out. Then to Will: "We don't have it, nor it seems have we ordered it. Would you like me to order a copy for you?" and he says "Truth is I'd like two copies, one for me, one for a friend. Can you get them in a relatively short time?" "I can if you pay for them first. You know, we've had miserable luck ordering books which the customers then don't come in to pay for or pick up or even bother to inform us that they're not interested in the book anymore. Very often it's the author himself who orders these books, or relatives or good friends of the author. That's just my assumption, of course, but one borne out from what other bookstores have told me. You're not this William Taub or a blood relative or good friend of his, are you? No, of course you're not—just joking. Would you like me to place that order for two copies? You'll have to come in and pay by cash, as I said, or else give me your credit card number over the phone if you'd prefer doing it that way." "No, I'll take my chances that another store has the book, but thank you."

He calls another bookstore and says "I was in your store two weeks ago—maybe three—but anyway, I asked one of the clerks there if he had a new novel by a good friend of mine, William Taub. The title's *Forewarned.*" "Yes? So?" the man says. "Well, the clerk said it was on order. Has it come in?" "William Taub's novel *Forewarned*? No, we don't have it...nor do I see any order for it. Did you pay for it by cash, credit card or charge?" "None of those. I didn't have to. The clerk said that copies of the book had been ordered a week before I even went into your store and that he'd phone me— he took my name and number—when the book came in." "P and P Bookshop you're talking about?" and Will says "P and P? No, I don't even know where that is. Everyman's Bookstore on Eighty-Sixth and Third. I'm sorry, I must have called the wrong store."

He calls another bookstore and says "About two weeks ago one of your clerks said—at the cash register—that a novel I inquired about, *Forewarned*, by William Taub, would be in in a few days and she'd call me, but she never did. Do you know if you got it in yet?" and the man says *Fore-warned?* Nobody here ordered that book." "This is Everyman's Bookshop, am I wrong?" and the man says "Bookstore, Everyman's Bookstore, you're right, but I'm the one who does all the ordering here and I'm certain I didn't order it. South Street Press. Publishing date was November or December. I know the book. You recall the name of the clerk who took care of you?" "No I don't. How can I? It was a woman though." "Around what age was she?" and Will says "Young, or not that young. Thirty-five I'd say, or a little less or more. Really, I can't even be sure of that. I wasn't paying much attention to her looks. I came in with my little girl—she was in a stroller—so my attention was going back and forth from the clerk, my child, the book, ordering, and so on. Maybe the clerk would remember me." "We only have two women salespersons in this store. One's quite young—Karen—and the other has been with us for almost thirty years and was around the age you say when she started here, so she's much older than the woman you even vaguely describe. But since you say it was Everyman's Bookstore you ordered this title from, I'm sitting here trying to figure out how the error could have been made and what to do about it now." "Maybe it wasn't Everyman's then—I was almost sure it was but I no longer am. I'd been out for about three hours with my baby that day, and between—you know—ducking in here and there, taking care of her, looking for an un-crowded luncheonette at the peak of the lunch hour when she suddenly got hungry and I realized I'd forgotten her food—it was around noon or one when I was in your store, or just a bookstore. Anyway, let's say yours wasn't the one on Madison I ordered the book from—" "We're right off Third, not Madison, on Eighty-Sixth." "Then I'm really confused—blocks away from where I thought I was. No, mine was—well now I'm not even sure what avenue it was on. Madison, I thought—the upper East Side I'm sure. Look, since I don't think I'll ever remember what store I ordered the book from, why don't I just ask if first, you have any copies of the book in stock, and if you don't, could you possibly order a couple of copies for me?" "We haven't the book but we can order any number of copies for you if you don't mind paying for them beforehand. Nothing personal to do with you, you understand, but we had a terrible time last year taking special orders over the phone—I'm not going to go into it— so we've discontinued that policy except for our oldest customers. What I suggest is you come in, if it's no inconvenience for you, pay for the books by cash or credit card, and we'll have them in a week or so and we'll even mail them to you if you also pay those mailing costs." "Actually, it would be a little inconvenient to come in in the next few days." "Then perhaps, not that I like steering business away from us, you'll have better luck ordering the book over the phone in one of the other stores around here. P and P, for instance. Or Greer's on Eighty-Third, Classics and Company on Lexington and Seventy-Fourth, or any of the three Ralston stores further downtown." "Thanks. That's a good idea. Maybe I will."

Only The Cat Escapes

M agna comes into the room. "Oh, Will, you're reading in bed. That's what I had decided to do. Would you mind if I joined you?"
"Come ahead."

She lies beside me on the bed and opens her book. I return to my book. She says after about a minute "Suppose I told you I don't want to read right now?"

"Let's say you just told me."

"That's what I meant. Suppose I did. What would you say?"

"I'd say 'What do you mean you don't want to read right now?'"

"And suppose I answered that I don't want to read right now because I have something else in mind?"

"Then I'd ask what that is."

"Let's say you have asked."

"Let's say I have."

"And let's say I then said I'd like to sleep with you right now."

"So?"

"Well, what's your reply?"

"My reply?" I put my book down and think. "My reply?" She puts her book on top of my book between us. Her cat jumps on the bed and lies on my feet. I say "Do you think your cat should be on the bed at a time like this?"

"What time is that?"

"A time when I'm about to say that I think it's a pretty good idea if we do sleep together right now."

"If you did say that then I'd say it probably isn't a good time for my cat to be on the bed."

"All right, let's say I said it."

"Then I suppose I should tell the cat to get off the bed."

"Why don't you?"

"I will."

Just then the cat jumps off the bed and runs underneath it.

"It seems," she says, "I didn't have to tell the cat to get off the bed."

"Seems so. But what next?"

"What next what? That I should do something about getting it out from under the bed and maybe even out of the room?"

"No, let it stay there, what's the harm? I mean about our sleeping together."

"About that I'd say I think we should start."

"And to that I'd say that I think we already did start when we began talking about it and put our books down."

"But we put our books down between us. That might end up being a little too uncomfortable for us if we actually do start sleeping with each other right now."

"'Sleeping' as whatever figure of speech it is for 'making love,' I suppose. I mean, that is what you had in mind when you said 'sleeping,' isn't it?"

"First making love, then maybe sleeping together on this bed if we like."

"That's what I thought." I take the books in one hand and drop them on the floor. The cat runs out from under the bed and down the stairs.

"I didn't intend, I want you to know, to scare the cat away by dropping the books."

"If you say so, then you didn't," she says.

"Didn't intend to."

"Right."

"But you did think I might have intended to scare it, isn't that so?"

"I thought you might have intended to, but I didn't worry about it much."

"You worried about it a little, though, no?"

"What happened was this. When you dropped the books and that cat ran out I thought for a second or two you might have intentionally scared my cat by dropping the books you were getting rid of for us and that that act could indicate something about your personality or nature or whatever it's called that I might not like about you. But it turned out not to be so. You didn't try to scare it. Or did you?"

"I didn't. I even forgot the cat was under the bed."

"Which I think is really, if I had had more time to think about it then, what I would have ended up thinking had happened. But where did we leave off after we stopped talking about figures of speech and sleeping together as meaning making love?"

"We left with that, I think. But are you saying you think we should try and carry on from that point?"

"Not try but do, if you still want to."

"Do you?"

"I'm sorry, but didn't I just say I did?"

"I do," I say.

"So do I."

"But if I had said I didn't, what would you have said?"

"I would have wondered why you didn't want to anymore."

"You would have wondered but would you have said it?"

"I might have. But because I do want to sleep with you or make love or both, I would have said it in a way which

wouldn't have done anything to discourage you from wanting to sleep with me or make love or both, or I at least would
have tried to say it in that way."

"What way would that be?"

"Gently. Sincerely. Lovingly, I suppose. Surely softly, if
that isn't the same thing as saying it gently. But you know.
I might have taken your hand." She takes my hand. "Like
this. My hand around yours. And then got up on my side, like
this, and said very gently and lovingly or not 'very' but just
gently and lovingly and the rest of those ways...what was it
I would have said? I forget."

"You mean before in response to my saying what would
you have said if I had said I didn't want to sleep or make love
with you or both anymore?"

"That's right. I would have said softly and sincerely, as
I'm doing, lovingly and gently, as I'm still doing, and with my
torso up on its side, as I've done and it still is, and my hands
where they are now, 'Why don't you want to sleep with me
or make love with me or do both with me now? Is it
something I said?'"

"You would have said 'Is it something I said?'"

"I would have, yes," she says. "And if I had said all that
in the way I said it and with my torso and hands the way they
still are, what would you have said and done to me?"

"I would have got up on my side, facing you, as I'm now
going to do, but carefully, so your hand wouldn't slip off my
neck—"

"It's okay. If it slips I can put it back."

"And with my other hand still in your hand, as it still is,
and also lovingly and sincerely and gently and softly, though
maybe not as gently and softly as you said it, since I don't
seem to be able to get my voice as gentle and soft as yours,
possibly because of our respective sexes and because of that,
our different vocal quality and tone. And maybe also be-

cause of our different personalities and sensibilities and backgrounds or something, though I don't know the physical and characteristical reasons why that should be so. But I would have said 'No, it wasn't anything you said. I simply don't want to make love or sleep with you right now, that's all.'"

She takes her hand off mine and other hand off my neck and says "You would have said that?"

"I wouldn't have."

"Then why'd you say it?"

"I didn't say it as if I meant it but just to see what your reaction would be like."

"And what would it be like?"

"Not 'would' but 'was.' You took both hands away from me but kept your torso on its side facing mine, and in a voice not as gentle and soft and loving as before but as sincere, you said 'You would have said that?'"

"Would you like to know why I reacted that way?"

"I can guess."

"Go ahead and guess then," she says.

"Because you probably believed that I didn't want to make love or sleep with you right now. Is that it?"

"I'm not saying."

"Can I ask how come?"

"You can ask."

"How come?"

"I'm not saying."

"Can I ask how come?"

"You already asked how come and I already said I'm not saying."

"That was to something else" I say. But can I make a guess why you're not saying anything to any of my questions?"

"Make a guess. But I won't tell you if your guess is

accurate or not."

"Can I ask how come?"

"Again, you can ask, but I'm not saying, I won't say, and that's that."

"You're not saying what?"

"I'm not saying, period."

"Why not? You answered all my other questions till now, if not directly then indirectly, but you gave me answers at least, just as I did to you in either of those two ways."

"I thought by me saying 'I'm not saying' I was giving an indirect answer. You didn't get it?"

"No. But now that I know it was an indirect answer, maybe it'll be easier to get. Give me time to think."

She takes my hand.

"I think I'm getting it," I say.

She puts her other hand on the back of my neck.

"Now I get it. Or I'm almost sure I got it."

"From now on I'll only say 'what?'" she says.

"You don't want to talk anymore?"

"What?"

"You just want to make love or sleep or some other figure of speech with me, but you think talking about it too much sort of kills it?"

"What? What?" She brings her lips close to mine.

"You want to kiss and take off my clothes or have me take them off and also your clothes off or you want to take off your clothes by yourself? You want us to do all that or some of those or more?"

"What? What? What?"

"You want me to turn off the light or make it less bright by turning off one or two of the lamp's three bulbs, and you also want us to get closer, not just our lips, and do other things with our bodies and more? Am I right?"

"What? What? What? What?"

"Just say I'm right."

"What? What? What?"

"I'm sure I'm almost right."

"What? What?"

"I'm going to have to turn around to turn off the light or to turn it down, all right?"

"What?"

I turn around to the lamp on the night table on my side of the bed. Her hand slides off my neck onto my hip. Her other hand stays around mine but she's squeezing it now when she wasn't before. Her face is no longer near mine but it probably will be again once I turn the light off or down and turn back around. I turn off all three bulbs. It's still daylight out but gray because of the clouds and rain, and the room's dark mostly because of the tall trees that surround the house. I turn around and face her. I can't see her face but can her form. She puts her hand back on my neck and her mouth close to mine. "I want—" I start to say, but she takes her hand off my neck and puts one finger across my lips to stop me from saying whatever I was going to say, which was "I want to tell you that I love you very very much," and takes her finger away and kisses my lips.

About the Author

STEPHEN DIXON is the author of about 300 published short stories, four novels and eight short story collections besides *Friends*. He lives in Baltimore with his wife, Anne Frydman, and two daughters, Sophia and Antonia, and teaches in the Writing Seminars at Johns Hopkins University. For those who are superstitious, *Friends* is his 13th book. Books by Mr. Dixon have appeared in Germany, Poland and France and stories of his have been widely anthologized. He held many jobs before he became a college teacher: waiter, bartender, department store salesman, tour leader, high school teacher, etc.

Mr. Dixon's novels are *Work* (1977), *Too Late* (1978), *Fall & Rise* (1985) and *Garbage* (1988). His story collections are *No Relief* (1976), *Quite Contrary* (1978), *14 Stories* (1980), *Movies* (1983), *Time To Go* (1985), *The Play* (1989), *Love and Will* (1989) and *All Gone* (1990).

He is presently working on a long work-in-progress called *Frog*, which is an interconnected collection of fictions composed of three novels, two novellas, and sixteen stories.